Samuel Langhorne Clemens (November 30, 1835 – April 21, 1910), known by his pen name Mark Twain, was an American writer, humorist, entrepreneur, publisher, and lecturer. He was lauded as the "greatest humorist this country has produced", and William Faulkner called him "the father of American literature". His novels include The Adventures of Tom Sawyer (1876) and its sequel, the Adventures of Huckleberry Finn (1884), the latter often called "The Great American Novel".

Twain was raised in Hannibal, Missouri, which later provided the setting for Tom Sawyer and Huckleberry Finn. He served an apprenticeship with a printer and then worked as a typesetter, contributing articles to the newspaper of his older brother Orion Clemens. He later became a riverboat pilot on the Mississippi River before heading west to join Orion in Nevada. (Source: Wikipedia)

Literary works:
The Gilded Age: A Tale of Today (1873)
The Prince and the Pauper (1881)
A Connecticut Yankee in
King Arthur's Court (1889)
The American Claimant (1892)
Pudd'nhead Wilson (1894)
Personal Recollections of Joan of Arc (1896)
A Horse's Tale (1907)
The Mysterious Stranger (1916, posthumous)
The Adventures of Tom Sawyer (1876)
Adventures of Huckleberry Finn (1884)
Tom Sawyer Abroad (1894)
Tom Sawyer, Detective (1896)
"Eve's Diary" (1906)

THE CURIOUS REPUBLIC OF GONDOUR AND OTHER WHIMSICAL SKETCHES
MARK TWAIN

PRINCE CLASSICS

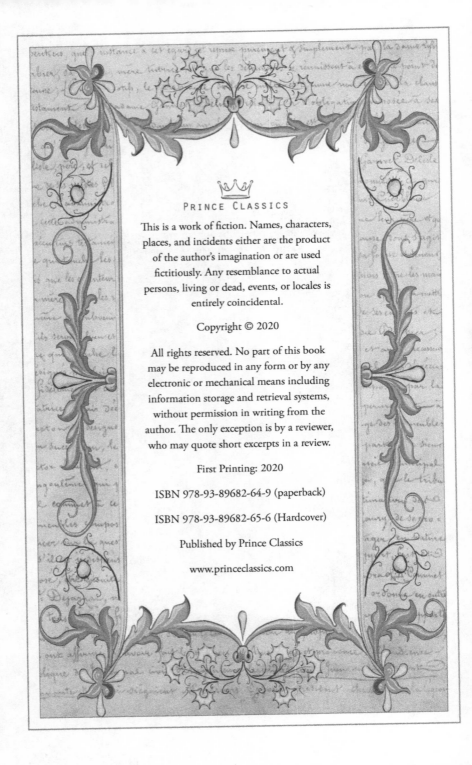

PRINCE CLASSICS

This is a work of fiction. Names, characters, places, and incidents either are the product of the author's imagination or are used fictitiously. Any resemblance to actual persons, living or dead, events, or locales is entirely coincidental.

Copyright © 2020

First Printing: 2020

ISBN 978-93-89682-64-9 (paperback)

ISBN 978-93-89682-65-6 (Hardcover)

Published by Prince Classics

www.princeclassics.com

Contents

THE CURIOUS REPUBLIC OF GONDOUR
AND OTHER WHIMSICAL SKETCHES

NOTE:

Most of the sketches in this volume were taken from a series

the author wrote for The Galaxy from May, 1870, to April,

1871. The rest appeared in The Buffalo Express.

THE CURIOUS REPUBLIC OF GONDOUR

As soon as I had learned to speak the language a little, I became greatly interested in the people and the system of government.

I found that the nation had at first tried universal suffrage pure and simple, but had thrown that form aside because the result was not satisfactory. It had seemed to deliver all power into the hands of the ignorant and non-tax-paying classes; and of a necessity the responsible offices were filled from these classes also.

A remedy was sought. The people believed they had found it; not in the destruction of universal suffrage, but in the enlargement of it. It was an odd idea, and ingenious. You must understand, the constitution gave every man a vote; therefore that vote was a vested right, and could not be taken away. But the constitution did not say that certain individuals might not be given two votes, or ten! So an amendatory clause was inserted in a quiet way; a clause which authorised the enlargement of the suffrage in certain cases to be specified by statute. To offer to "limit" the suffrage might have made instant trouble; the offer to "enlarge" it had a pleasant aspect. But of course the newspapers soon began to suspect; and then out they came! It was found, however, that for once—and for the first time in the history of the republic— property, character, and intellect were able to wield a political influence; for once, money, virtue, and intelligence took a vital and a united interest in a political question; for once these powers went to the "primaries" in strong force; for once the best men in the nation were put forward as candidates for that parliament whose business it should be to enlarge the suffrage. The weightiest half of the press quickly joined forces with the new movement, and left the other half to rail about the proposed "destruction of the liberties" of the bottom layer of society, the hitherto governing class of the community.

The victory was complete. The new law was framed and passed. Under it every citizen, howsoever poor or ignorant, possessed one vote, so universal suffrage still reigned; but if a man possessed a good common-school education and no money, he had two votes; a high-school education gave him four; if he had property likewise, to the value of three thousand 'sacos,' he wielded one more vote; for every fifty thousand 'sacos' a man added to his property, he was entitled to another vote; a university education entitled a man to nine votes, even though he owned no property. Therefore, learning being more prevalent and more easily acquired than riches, educated men became a wholesome check upon wealthy men, since they could outvote them. Learning goes usually with uprightness, broad views, and humanity; so the learned voters, possessing the balance of power, became the vigilant and efficient protectors of the great lower rank of society.

And now a curious thing developed itself—a sort of emulation, whose object was voting power! Whereas formerly a man was honored only according to the amount of money he possessed, his grandeur was measured now by the number of votes he wielded. A man with only one vote was conspicuously respectful to his neighbor who possessed three. And if he was a man above the common-place, he was as conspicuously energetic in his determination to acquire three for himself. This spirit of emulation invaded all ranks. Votes based upon capital were commonly called "mortal" votes, because they could be lost; those based upon learning were called "immortal," because they were permanent, and because of their customarily imperishable character they were naturally more valued than the other sort. I say "customarily" for the reason that these votes were not absolutely imperishable, since insanity could suspend them.

Under this system, gambling and speculation almost ceased in the republic. A man honoured as the possessor of great voting power could not afford to risk the loss of it upon a doubtful chance.

It was curious to observe the manners and customs which the enlargement plan produced. Walking the street with a friend one day he delivered a careless bow to a passer-by, and then remarked that that person possessed only one vote and would probably never earn another; he was more respectful to the next acquaintance he met; he explained that this salute was a four-vote bow. I tried to "average" the importance of the people he accosted after that, by the nature of his bows, but my success was only partial, because of the somewhat greater homage paid to the immortals than to the mortals. My friend explained. He said there was no law to regulate this thing, except that most powerful of all laws, custom. Custom had created these varying bows, and in time they had become easy and natural. At this moment he delivered himself of a very profound salute, and then said, "Now there's a man who began life as a shoemaker's apprentice, and without education; now he swings twenty-two mortal votes and two immortal ones; he expects to pass a high-school examination this year and climb a couple of votes higher among the immortals; mighty valuable citizen."

By and by my friend met a venerable personage, and not only made him a most elaborate bow, but also took off his hat. I took off mine, too, with a mysterious awe. I was beginning to be infected.

"What grandee is that?"

"That is our most illustrious astronomer. He hasn't any money, but is fearfully learned. Nine immortals is his political weight! He would swing a hundred and fifty votes if our system were perfect."

"Is there any altitude of mere moneyed grandeur that you take off your hat to?"

"No. Nine immortal votes is the only power we uncover for—that is, in civil life. Very great officials receive that mark of homage, of course."

It was common to hear people admiringly mention men who had begun life on the lower levels and in time achieved great voting-power. It was also common to hear youths planning a future of ever so many votes for themselves. I heard shrewd mammas speak of certain young men as good "catches" because they possessed such-and-such a number of votes. I knew of more than one case where an heiress was married to a youngster who had but one vote; the argument being that he was gifted with such excellent parts that in time he would acquire a good voting strength, and perhaps in the long run be able to outvote his wife, if he had luck.

Competitive examinations were the rule and in all official grades. I remarked that the questions asked the candidates were wild, intricate, and often required a sort of knowledge not needed in the office sought.

"Can a fool or an ignoramus answer them?" asked the person I was talking with.

"Certainly not."

"Well, you will not find any fools or ignoramuses among our officials."

I felt rather cornered, but made shift to say:—

"But these questions cover a good deal more ground than is necessary."

"No matter; if candidates can answer these it is tolerably fair evidence that they can answer nearly any other question you choose to ask them."

There were some things in Gondour which one could not shut his eyes to. One was, that ignorance and incompetence had no place in the government. Brains and property managed the state. A candidate for office must have marked ability, education, and high character, or he stood no sort of chance of election. If a hod-carrier possessed these, he could succeed; but the mere fact that he was a hod-carrier could not elect him, as in previous times.

It was now a very great honour to be in the parliament or in office; under the old system such distinction had only brought suspicion upon a man and made him a helpless mark for newspaper contempt and scurrility. Officials did not need to steal now, their salaries being vast in comparison with the pittances paid in the days when parliaments were created by hod-carriers, who viewed official salaries from a hod-carrying point of view and compelled that view to be respected by their obsequious servants. Justice was wisely and rigidly administered; for a judge, after once reaching his place through the specified line of promotions, was a permanency during good behaviour. He was not obliged to modify his judgments according to the effect they might have upon the temper of a reigning political party.

The country was mainly governed by a ministry which went out with the administration that created it. This was also the case with the chiefs of the great departments. Minor officials ascended to their several positions through well-earned promotions, and not by a jump from gin-mills or the needy families and friends of members of parliament. Good behaviour measured their terms of office.

The head of the government, the Grand Caliph, was elected for a term of twenty years. I questioned the wisdom of this. I was answered that he could do no harm, since the ministry and the parliament governed the land, and he was liable to impeachment for misconduct. This great office had twice been ably filled by women, women as aptly fitted for it as some of the sceptred queens of history. Members of the cabinet, under many administrations, had been women.

I found that the pardoning power was lodged in a court of pardons, consisting of several great judges. Under the old regime, this important power was vested in a single official, and he usually took care to have a general jail delivery in time for the next election.

I inquired about public schools. There were plenty of them, and of free colleges too. I inquired about compulsory education. This was received with a smile, and the remark:—

"When a man's child is able to make himself powerful and honoured according to the amount of education he acquires, don't you suppose that that parent will apply the compulsion himself? Our free schools and free colleges require no law to fill them."

There was a loving pride of country about this person's way of speaking which annoyed me. I had long been unused to the sound of it in my own. The Gondour national airs were forever dinning in my ears; therefore I was glad to leave that country and come back to my dear native land, where one never hears that sort of music.

A MEMORY

When I say that I never knew my austere father to be enamoured of but one poem in all the long half century that he lived, persons who knew him will easily believe me; when I say that I have never composed but one poem in all the long third of a century that I have lived, persons who know me will be sincerely grateful; and finally, when I say that the poem which I composed was not the one which my father was enamoured of, persons who may have known us both will not need to have this truth shot into them with a mountain howitzer before they can receive it. My father and I were always on the most distant terms when I was a boy—a sort of armed neutrality so to speak. At irregular intervals this neutrality was broken, and suffering ensued; but I will be candid enough to say that the breaking and the suffering were always divided up with strict impartiality between us—which is to say, my father did the breaking, and I did the suffering. As a general thing I was a backward, cautious, unadventurous boy; but I once jumped off a two-story table; another time I gave an elephant a "plug" of tobacco and retired without waiting for an answer; and still another time I pretended to be talking in my sleep, and got off a portion of a very wretched original conundrum in the hearing of my father. Let us not pry into the result; it was of no consequence to any one but me.

But the poem I have referred to as attracting my father's attention and achieving his favour was "Hiawatha." Some man who courted a sudden and awful death presented him an early copy, and I never lost faith in my own senses until I saw him sit down and go to reading it in cold blood—saw him open the book, and heard him read these following lines, with the same inflectionless judicial frigidity with which he always read his charge to the jury, or administered an oath to a witness:

> "*Take your bow,*
>
> *O Hiawatha,*
>
> *Take your arrows, jasper-headed,*

> *Take your war-club, Puggawaugun,*
>
> *And your mittens, Minjekahwan,*
>
> *And your birch canoe for sailing,*
>
> *And the oil of Mishe-Nama."*

Presently my father took out of his breast pocket an imposing "Warranty Deed," and fixed his eyes upon it and dropped into meditation. I knew what it was. A Texan lady and gentleman had given my half-brother, Orrin Johnson, a handsome property in a town in the North, in gratitude to him for having saved their lives by an act of brilliant heroism.

By and by my father looked towards me and sighed. Then he said:

"If I had such a son as this poet, here were a subject worthier than the traditions of these Indians."

"If you please, sir, where?"

"In this deed."

"Yes—in this very deed," said my father, throwing it on the table. "There is more poetry, more romance, more sublimity, more splendid imagery hidden away in that homely document than could be found in all the traditions of all the savages that live."

"Indeed, sir? Could I—could I get it out, sir? Could I compose the poem, sir, do you think?"

"You?"

I wilted.

Presently my father's face softened somewhat, and he said:

"Go and try. But mind, curb folly. No poetry at the expense of truth. Keep strictly to the facts."

I said I would, and bowed myself out, and went upstairs.

"Hiawatha" kept droning in my head—and so did my father's remarks about the sublimity and romance hidden in my subject, and also his injunction to beware of wasteful and exuberant fancy. I noticed, just here, that I had heedlessly brought the deed away with me; now at this moment came to me one of those rare moods of daring recklessness, such as I referred to a while ago. Without another thought, and in plain defiance of the fact that I knew my father meant me to write the romantic story of my half-brother's adventure and subsequent good fortune, I ventured to heed merely the letter of his remarks and ignore their spirit. I took the stupid "Warranty Deed" itself and chopped it up into Hiawathian blank verse without altering or leaving out three words, and without transposing six. It required loads of courage to go downstairs and face my father with my performance. I started three or four times before I finally got my pluck to where it would stick. But at last I said I would go down and read it to him if he threw me over the church for it. I stood up to begin, and he told me to come closer. I edged up a little, but still left as much neutral ground between us as I thought he would stand. Then I began. It would be useless for me to try to tell what conflicting emotions expressed themselves upon his face, nor how they grew more and more intense, as I proceeded; nor how a fell darkness descended upon his countenance, and he began to gag and swallow, and his hands began to work and twitch, as I reeled off line after line, with the strength ebbing out of me, and my legs trembling under me:

THE STORY OF A GALLANT DEED

THIS INDENTURE, made the tenth

Day of November, in the year

Of our Lord one thousand eight

Hundred six-and-fifty,

Between Joanna S. E. Gray

And Philip Gray, her husband,

Of Salem City in the State

Of Texas, of the first part,

And O. B. Johnson, of the town

Of Austin, ditto, WITNESSETH:

That said party of first part,

For and in consideration

Of the sum of Twenty Thousand

Dollars, lawful money of

The U. S. of Americay,

To them in hand now paid by said

Party of the second part,

The due receipt whereof is here—

By confessed and acknowledged

Having Granted, Bargained, Sold, Remised,

Released and Aliened and Conveyed,

Confirmed, and by these presents do

Grant and Bargain, Sell, Remise,

Alien, Release, Convey, and Con—

Firm unto the said aforesaid

Party of the second part,

And to his heirs and assigns

Forever and ever ALL

That certain lot or parcel of

LAND situate in city of

Dunkirk, County of Chautauqua,

And likewise furthermore in York State

Bounded and described, to-wit,

As follows, herein, namely

BEGINNING at the distance of

A hundred two-and-forty feet,

North-half-east, north-east-by north,

East-north-east and northerly

Of the northerly line of Mulligan street

On the westerly line of Brannigan street,

And running thence due northerly

On Brannigan street 200 feet,

Thence at right angles westerly,

North-west-by-west-and-west-half-west,

West-and-by-north, north-west-by-west,

About—

I kind of dodged, and the boot-jack broke the looking-glass. I could have waited to see what became of the other missiles if I had wanted to, but I took no interest in such things.

INTRODUCTORY TO "MEMORANDA"

In taking upon myself the burden of editing a department in THE GALAXY magazine, I have been actuated by a conviction that I was needed, almost imperatively, in this particular field of literature. I have long felt that while the magazine literature of the day had much to recommend it, it yet lacked stability, solidity, weight. It seemed plain to me that too much space was given to poetry and romance, and not enough to statistics and agriculture. This defect it shall be my earnest endeavour to remedy. If I succeed, the simple consciousness that I have done a good deed will be a sufficient reward.**— [**Together with salary.]

In this department of mine the public may always rely upon finding exhaustive statistical tables concerning the finances of the country, the ratio of births and deaths; the percentage of increase of population, etc., etc.—in a word, everything in the realm of statistics that can make existence bright and beautiful.

Also, in my department will always be found elaborate condensations of the Patent Office Reports, wherein a faithful endeavour will at all times be made to strip the nutritious facts bare of that effulgence of imagination and sublimity of diction which too often mar the excellence of those great works.**

*[** N. B.—No other magazine in the country makes a*

specialty of the Patent Office Reports.]

In my department will always be found ample excerpts from those able dissertations upon Political Economy which I have for a long time been contributing to a great metropolitan journal, and which, for reasons utterly incomprehensible to me, another party has chosen to usurp the credit of composing.

And, finally, I call attention with pride to the fact that in my department of the magazine the farmer will always find full market reports, and also complete instructions about farming, even from the grafting of the seed to the harrowing of the matured crop. I shall throw a pathos into the subject of Agriculture that will surprise and delight the world.

Such is my programme; and I am persuaded that by adhering to it with fidelity I shall succeed in materially changing the character of this magazine. Therefore I am emboldened to ask the assistance and encouragement of all whose sympathies are with Progress and Reform.

In the other departments of the magazine will be found poetry, tales, and other frothy trifles, and to these the reader can turn for relaxation from time to time, and thus guard against overstraining the powers of his mind. M. T.

P. S.—1. I have not sold out of the "Buffalo Express," and shall not; neither shall I stop writing for it. This remark seems necessary in a business point of view.

2. These MEMORANDA are not a "humorous" department. I would not conduct an exclusively and professedly humorous department for any one. I would always prefer to have the privilege of printing a serious and sensible remark, in case one occurred to me, without the reader's feeling obliged to consider himself outraged. We cannot keep the same mood day after day. I am liable, some day, to want to print my opinion on jurisprudence, or Homeric poetry, or international law, and I shall do it. It will be of small consequence to me whether the reader survive or not. I shall never go straining after jokes when in a cheerless mood, so long as the unhackneyed subject of international law is open to me. I will leave all that straining to people who edit professedly and inexorably "humorous" departments and publications.

3. I have chosen the general title of MEMORANDA for this department because it is plain and simple, and makes no fraudulent promises. I can print under it statistics, hotel arrivals, or anything that comes handy, without violating faith with the reader.

4. Puns cannot be allowed a place in this department. Inoffensive ignorance, benignant stupidity, and unostentatious imbecility will always be

welcomed and cheerfully accorded a corner, and even the feeblest humour will be admitted, when we can do no better; but no circumstances, however dismal, will ever be considered a sufficient excuse for the admission of that last—and saddest evidence of intellectual poverty, the Pun.

ABOUT SMELLS

In a recent issue of the "Independent," the Rev. T. De Witt Talmage, of Brooklyn, has the following utterance on the subject of "Smells":

I have a good Christian friend who, if he sat in the front pew in church, and a working man should enter the door at the other end, would smell him instantly. My friend is not to blame for the sensitiveness of his nose, any more than you would flog a pointer for being keener on the scent than a stupid watch dog. The fact is, if you had all the churches free, by reason of the mixing up of the common people with the uncommon, you would keep one-half of Christendom sick at their stomach. If you are going to kill the church thus with bad smells, I will have nothing to do with this work of evangelization.

We have reason to believe that there will be labouring men in heaven; and also a number of negroes, and Esquimaux, and Terra del Fuegans, and Arabs, and a few Indians, and possibly even some Spaniards and Portuguese. All things are possible with God. We shall have all these sorts of people in heaven; but, alas! in getting them we shall lose the society of Dr. Talmage. Which is to say, we shall lose the company of one who could give more real "tone" to celestial society than any other contribution Brooklyn could furnish. And what would eternal happiness be without the Doctor? Blissful, unquestionably—we know that well enough—but would it be 'distingue,' would it be 'recherche' without him? St. Matthew without stockings or sandals; St. Jerome bare headed, and with a coarse brown blanket robe dragging the ground; St. Sebastian with scarcely any raiment at all—these we should see, and should enjoy seeing them; but would we not miss a spike-tailed coat and kids, and turn away regretfully, and say to parties from the Orient: "These are well enough, but you ought to see Talmage of Brooklyn." I fear me that in the better world we shall not even have Dr. Talmage's "good Christian friend."

For if he were sitting under the glory of the Throne, and the keeper of the keys admitted a Benjamin Franklin or other labouring man, that "friend," with his fine natural powers infinitely augmented by emancipation from hampering flesh, would detect him with a single sniff, and immediately take his hat and ask to be excused.

To all outward seeming, the Rev. T. De Witt Talmage is of the same material as that used in the construction of his early predecessors in the ministry; and yet one feels that there must be a difference somewhere between him and the Saviour's first disciples. It may be because here, in the nineteenth century, Dr. T. has had advantages which Paul and Peter and the others could not and did not have. There was a lack of polish about them, and a looseness of etiquette, and a want of exclusiveness, which one cannot help noticing. They healed the very beggars, and held intercourse with people of a villainous odour every day. If the subject of these remarks had been chosen among the original Twelve Apostles, he would not have associated with the rest, because he could not have stood the fishy smell of some of his comrades who came from around the Sea of Galilee. He would have resigned his commission with some such remark as he makes in the extract quoted above: "Master, if thou art going to kill the church thus with bad smells, I will have nothing to do with this work of evangelization." He is a disciple, and makes that remark to the Master; the only difference is, that he makes it in the nineteenth instead of the first century.

Is there a choir in Mr. T.'s church? And does it ever occur that they have no better manners than to sing that hymn which is so suggestive of labourers and mechanics:

> *"Son of the Carpenter! receive*
>
> *This humble work of mine?"*

Now, can it be possible that in a handful of centuries the Christian character has fallen away from an imposing heroism that scorned even the stake, the cross, and the axe, to a poor little effeminacy that withers and wilts under an unsavoury smell? We are not prepared to believe so, the reverend Doctor and his friend to the contrary notwithstanding.

A COUPLE OF SAD EXPERIENCES

When I published a squib recently in which I said I was going to edit an Agricultural Department in this magazine, I certainly did not desire to deceive anybody. I had not the remotest desire to play upon any one's confidence with a practical joke, for he is a pitiful creature indeed who will degrade the dignity of his humanity to the contriving of the witless inventions that go by that name. I purposely wrote the thing as absurdly and as extravagantly as it could be written, in order to be sure and not mislead hurried or heedless readers: for I spoke of launching a triumphal barge upon a desert, and planting a tree of prosperity in a mine—a tree whose fragrance should slake the thirst of the naked, and whose branches should spread abroad till they washed the chorea of, etc., etc. I thought that manifest lunacy like that would protect the reader. But to make assurance absolute, and show that I did not and could not seriously mean to attempt an Agricultural Department, I stated distinctly in my postscript that I did not know anything about Agriculture. But alas! right there is where I made my worst mistake—for that remark seems to have recommended my proposed Agriculture more than anything else. It lets a little light in on me, and I fancy I perceive that the farmers feel a little bored, sometimes, by the oracular profundity of agricultural editors who "know it all." In fact, one of my correspondents suggests this (for that unhappy squib has deluged me with letters about potatoes, and cabbages, and hominy, and vermicelli, and maccaroni, and all the other fruits, cereals, and vegetables that ever grew on earth; and if I get done answering questions about the best way of raising these things before I go raving crazy, I shall be thankful, and shall never write obscurely for fun any more).

Shall I tell the real reason why I have unintentionally succeeded in fooling so many people? It is because some of them only read a little of the squib I wrote and jumped to the conclusion that it was serious, and the rest did not read it at all, but heard of my agricultural venture at second-hand. Those cases I could not guard against, of course. To write a burlesque so wild that its pretended facts will not be accepted in perfect good faith by somebody, is very nearly an impossible thing to do. It is because, in some instances, the reader is a person who never tries to deceive anybody himself, and therefore is not expecting any one to wantonly practise a deception upon him; and in this case the only person dishonoured is the man who wrote the burlesque. In other instances the "nub" or moral of the burlesque—if its object be to enforce a truth—escapes notice in the superior glare of something in the body of the burlesque itself. And very often this "moral" is tagged on at the bottom, and the reader, not knowing that it is the key of the whole thing and the only important paragraph in the article, tranquilly turns up his nose at it and leaves it unread. One can deliver a satire with telling force through the insidious medium of a travesty, if he is careful not to overwhelm the satire with the extraneous interest of the travesty, and so bury it from the reader's sight and leave him a joked and defrauded victim, when the honest intent was to add to either his knowledge or his wisdom. I have had a deal of experience in burlesques and their unfortunate aptness to deceive the public, and this is why I tried hard to make that agricultural one so broad and so perfectly palpable that even a one-eyed potato could see it; and yet, as I speak the solemn truth, it fooled one of the ablest agricultural editors in America!

DAN MURPHY

One of the saddest things that ever came under my notice (said the banker's clerk) was there in Corning, during the war. Dan Murphy enlisted as a private, and fought very bravely. The boys all liked him, and when a wound by and by weakened him down till carrying a musket was too heavy work for him, they clubbed together and fixed him up as a sutler. He made money then, and sent it always to his wife to bank for him. She was a washer and ironer, and knew enough by hard experience to keep money when she got it. She didn't waste a penny. On the contrary, she began to get miserly as her bank account grew. She grieved to part with a cent, poor creature, for twice in her hard-working life she had known what it was to be hungry, cold, friendless, sick, and without a dollar in the world, and she had a haunting dread of suffering so again. Well, at last Dan died; and the boys, in testimony of their esteem and respect for him, telegraphed to Mrs. Murphy to know if she would like to have him embalmed and sent home, when you know the usual custom was to dump a poor devil like him into a shallow hole, and then inform his friends what had become of him. Mrs. Murphy jumped to the conclusion that it would only cost two or three dollars to embalm her dead husband, and so she telegraphed "Yes." It was at the "wake" that the bill for embalming arrived and was presented to the widow. She uttered a wild, sad wail, that pierced every heart, and said: "Sivinty-foive dollars for stoofhn' Dan, blister their sowls! Did thim divils suppose I was goin' to stairt a Museim, that I'd be dalin' in such expinsive curiassities!"

The banker's clerk said there was not a dry eye in the house.

THE "TOURNAMENT" IN A. D. 1870

Lately there appeared an item to this effect, and the same went the customary universal round of the press:

> *A telegraph station has just been established upon the traditional site of the Garden of Eden.*

As a companion to that, nothing fits so aptly and so perfectly as this:

> *Brooklyn has revived the knightly tournament of the Middle Ages.*

It is hard to tell which is the most startling, the idea of that highest achievement of human genius and intelligence, the telegraph, prating away about the practical concerns of the world's daily life in the heart and home of ancient indolence, ignorance, and savagery, or the idea of that happiest expression of the brag, vanity, and mock-heroics of our ancestors, the "tournament," coming out of its grave to flaunt its tinsel trumpery and perform its "chivalrous" absurdities in the high noon of the nineteenth century, and under the patronage of a great, broad-awake city and an advanced civilisation.

A "tournament" in Lynchburg is a thing easily within the comprehension of the average mind; but no commonly gifted person can conceive of such a spectacle in Brooklyn without straining his powers. Brooklyn is part and parcel of the city of New York, and there is hardly romance enough in the entire metropolis to re-supply a Virginia "knight" with "chivalry," in case he happened to run out of it. Let the reader calmly and dispassionately picture to himself "lists"—in Brooklyn; heralds, pursuivants, pages, garter king-at-arms—in Brooklyn; the marshalling of the fantastic hosts of "chivalry" in slashed doublets, velvet trunks, ruffles, and plumes—in Brooklyn; mounted on omnibus and livery-stable patriarchs, promoted, and referred to in cold blood as "steeds," "destriers," and "chargers," and divested of their friendly, humble names—these meek old "Jims" and "Bobs" and "Charleys," and renamed "Mohammed," "Bucephalus," and "Saladin"—in Brooklyn; mounted thus, and armed with swords and shields and wooden lances, and cased in paste board hauberks, morions, greaves, and gauntlets, and addressed as "Sir" Smith, and "Sir" Jones, and bearing such titled grandeurs as "The Disinherited Knight," the "Knight of Shenandoah," the "Knight of the Blue Ridge," the "Knight of Maryland," and the "Knight of the Secret Sorrow"— in Brooklyn; and at the toot of the horn charging fiercely upon a helpless ring hung on a post, and prodding at it intrepidly with their wooden sticks, and by and by skewering it and cavorting back to the judges' stand covered with glory—this in Brooklyn; and each noble success like this duly and promptly announced by an applauding toot from the herald's horn, and "the band playing three bars of an old circus tune"—all in Brooklyn, in broad daylight. And let the reader remember, and also add to his picture, as follows, to wit: when the show was all over, the party who had shed the most blood and overturned and hacked to pieces the most knights, or at least had prodded the most muffin-rings, was accorded the ancient privilege of naming and crowning the Queen of Love and Beauty—which naming had in reality been done for him by the "cut-and-dried" process, and long in advance, by a committee of ladies, but the crowning he did in person, though suffering from loss of blood, and then was taken to the county hospital on a shutter to have his wounds dressed—these curious things all occurring in Brooklyn, and no longer ago than one or two yesterdays. It seems impossible, and yet it is true.

This was doubtless the first appearance of the "tournament" up here among the rolling-mills and factories, and will probably be the last. It will be well to let it retire permanently to the rural districts of Virginia, where, it is said, the fine mailed and plumed, noble-natured, maiden-rescuing, wrong-redressing, adventure-seeking knight of romance is accepted and believed in by the peasantry with pleasing simplicity, while they reject with scorn the plain, unpolished verdict whereby history exposes him as a braggart, a ruffian, a fantastic vagabond; and an ignoramus.

All romance aside, what shape would our admiration of the heroes of Ashby de la Zouch be likely to take, in this practical age, if those worthies were to rise up and come here and perform again the chivalrous deeds of that famous passage of arms? Nothing but a New York jury and the insanity plea could save them from hanging, from the amiable Bois-Guilbert and the pleasant Front-de-Boeuf clear down to the nameless ruffians that entered the riot with unpictured shields and did their first murder and acquired their first claim to respect that day. The doings of the so-called "chivalry" of the Middle Ages were absurd enough, even when they were brutally and bloodily in earnest, and when their surroundings of castles and donjons, savage landscapes and half-savage peoples, were in keeping; but those doings gravely reproduced with tinsel decorations and mock pageantry, by bucolic gentlemen with broomstick lances, and with muffin-rings to represent the foe, and all in the midst of the refinement and dignity of a carefully-developed modern civilisation, is absurdity gone crazy.

Now, for next exhibition, let us have a fine representation of one of those chivalrous wholesale butcheries and burnings of Jewish women and children, which the crusading heroes of romance used to indulge in in their European homes, just before starting to the Holy Land, to seize and take to their protection the Sepulchre and defend it from "pollution."

CURIOUS RELIC FOR SALE

"For sale, for the benefit of the Fund for the Relief of the Widows and Orphans of Deceased Firemen, a Curious Ancient Bedouin Pipe, procured at the city of Endor in Palestine, and believed to have once belonged to the justly-renowned Witch of Endor. Parties desiring to examine this singular relic with a view to purchasing, can do so by calling upon Daniel S., 119 and 121 William street, New York"

As per advertisement in the "Herald." A curious old relic indeed, as I had a good personal right to know. In a single instant of time, a long drawn panorama of sights and scenes in the Holy Land flashed through my memory—town and grove, desert, camp, and caravan clattering after each other and disappearing, leaving me with a little of the surprised and dizzy feeling which I have experienced at sundry times when a long express train has overtaken me at some quiet curve and gone whizzing, car by car, around the corner and out of sight. In that prolific instant I saw again all the country from the Sea of Galilee and Nazareth clear to Jerusalem, and thence over the hills of Judea and through the Vale of Sharon to Joppa, down by the ocean. Leaving out unimportant stretches of country and details of incident, I saw and experienced the following described matters and things. Immediately three years fell away from my age, and a vanished time was restored to me— September, 1867. It was a flaming Oriental day—this one that had come up out of the past and brought along its actors, its stage-properties, and scenic effects—and our party had just ridden through the squalid hive of human vermin which still holds the ancient Biblical name of Endor; I was bringing up the rear on my grave four-dollar steed, who was about beginning to compose himself for his usual noon nap. My! only fifteen minutes before how the black, mangy, nine-tenths naked, ten-tenths filthy, ignorant, bigoted, besotted, hungry, lazy, malignant, screeching, crowding, struggling, wailing, begging, cursing, hateful spawn of the original Witch had swarmed out of the caves in the rocks and the holes and crevices in the earth, and blocked our horses' way, besieged us, threw themselves in the animals' path, clung to their manes, saddle-furniture, and tails, asking, beseeching, demanding "bucksheesh! bucksheesh! BUCKSHEESH!" We had rained small copper Turkish coins among them, as fugitives fling coats and hats to pursuing wolves, and then had spurred our way through as they stopped to scramble for the largess. I was fervently thankful when we had gotten well up on the desolate hillside and outstripped them and left them jawing and gesticulating in the rear. What a tempest had seemingly gone roaring and crashing by me and left its dull thunders pulsing in my ears!

I was in the rear, as I was saying. Our pack-mules and Arabs were far ahead, and Dan, Jack, Moult, Davis, Denny, Church, and Birch (these names will do as well as any to represent the boys) were following close after them. As my horse nodded to rest, I heard a sort of panting behind me, and turned and saw that a tawny youth from the village had overtaken me—a true remnant and representative of his ancestress the Witch—a galvanised scurvy, wrought into the human shape and garnished with ophthalmia and leprous scars—an airy creature with an invisible shirt-front that reached below the pit of his stomach, and no other clothing to speak of except a tobacco-pouch, an ammunition-pocket, and a venerable gun, which was long enough to club any game with that came within shooting distance, but far from efficient as an article of dress.

I thought to myself, "Now this disease with a human heart in it is going to shoot me." I smiled in derision at the idea of a Bedouin daring to touch off his great-grandfather's rusty gun and getting his head blown off for his pains. But then it occurred to me, in simple school-boy language, "Suppose he should take deliberate aim and 'haul off' and fetch me with the butt-end of it?" There was wisdom in that view of it, and I stopped to parley. I found he was only a friendly villain who wanted a trifle of bucksheesh, and after begging what he could get in that way, was perfectly willing to trade off everything he had for more. I believe he would have parted with his last shirt for bucksheesh if he had had one. He was smoking the "humbliest" pipe I ever saw—a dingy, funnel-shaped, red-clay thing, streaked and grimed with oil and tears of tobacco, and with all the different kinds of dirt there are, and thirty per cent. of them peculiar and indigenous to Endor and perdition. And rank? I never smelt anything like it. It withered a cactus that stood lifting its prickly hands aloft beside the trail. It even woke up my horse. I said I would take that. It cost me a franc, a Russian kopek, a brass button, and a slate pencil; and my spendthrift lavishness so won upon the son of the desert that he passed over his pouch of most unspeakably villainous tobacco to me as a free gift. What a pipe it was, to be sure! It had a rude brass-wire cover to it, and a little coarse iron chain suspended from the bowl, with an iron splinter attached to loosen up the tobacco and pick your teeth with. The stem looked like the half of a slender walking-stick with the bark on.

I felt that this pipe had belonged to the original Witch of Endor as soon as I saw it; and as soon as I smelt it, I knew it. Moreover, I asked the Arab cub in good English if it was not so, and he answered in good Arabic that it was. I woke up my horse and went my way, smoking. And presently I said to myself reflectively, "If there is anything that could make a man deliberately assault a dying cripple, I reckon may be an unexpected whiff from this pipe would do it." I smoked along till I found I was beginning to lie, and project murder, and steal my own things out of one pocket and hide them in another; and then I put up my treasure, took off my spurs and put them under my horse's tail, and shortly came tearing through our caravan like a hurricane.

From that time forward, going to Jerusalem, the Dead Sea, and the Jordan, Bethany, Bethlehem, and everywhere, I loafed contentedly in the rear and enjoyed my infamous pipe and revelled in imaginary villany. But at the end of two weeks we turned our faces toward the sea and journeyed over the Judean hills, and through rocky defiles, and among the scenes that Samson knew in his youth, and by and by we touched level ground just at night, and trotted off cheerily over the plain of Sharon. It was perfectly jolly for three hours, and we whites crowded along together, close after the chief Arab muleteer (all the pack-animals and the other Arabs were miles in the rear), and we laughed, and chatted, and argued hotly about Samson, and

whether suicide was a sin or not, since Paul speaks of Samson distinctly as
being saved and in heaven. But by and by the night air, and the duskiness,
and the weariness of eight hours in the saddle, began to tell, and conversation
flagged and finally died out utterly. The squeak-squeaking of the saddles
grew very distinct; occasionally somebody sighed, or started to hum a tune
and gave it up; now and then a horse sneezed. These things only emphasised
the solemnity and the stillness. Everybody got so listless that for once I and
my dreamer found ourselves in the lead. It was a glad, new sensation, and I
longed to keep the place forevermore. Every little stir in the dingy cavalcade
behind made me nervous. Davis and I were riding side by side, right after
the Arab. About 11 o'clock it had become really chilly, and the dozing boys
roused up and began to inquire how far it was to Ramlah yet, and to demand
that the Arab hurry along faster. I gave it up then, and my heart sank within
me, because of course they would come up to scold the Arab. I knew I had to
take the rear again. In my sorrow I unconsciously took to my pipe, my only
comfort. As I touched the match to it the whole company came lumbering
up and crowding my horse's rump and flanks. A whiff of smoke drifted back
over my shoulder, and—

"The suffering Moses!"

"Whew!"

"By George, who opened that graveyard?"

"Boys, that Arab's been swallowing something dead!"

Right away there was a gap behind us. Whiff after whiff sailed airily
back, and each one widened the breach. Within fifteen seconds the barking,
and gasping, and sneezing, and coughing of the boys, and their angry abuse of
the Arab guide, had dwindled to a murmur, and Davis and I were alone with
the leader. Davis did not know what the matter was, and don't to this day.
Occasionally he caught a faint film of the smoke and fell to scolding at the
Arab and wondering how long he had been decaying in that way. Our boys
kept on dropping back further and further, till at last they were only in hearing,
not in sight. And every time they started gingerly forward to reconnoitre—or
shoot the Arab, as they proposed to do—I let them get within good fair range

of my relic (she would carry seventy yards with wonderful precision), and then wafted a whiff among them that sent them gasping and strangling to the rear again. I kept my gun well charged and ready, and twice within the hour I decoyed the boys right up to my horse's tail, and then with one malarious blast emptied the saddles, almost. I never heard an Arab abused so in my life. He really owed his preservation to me, because for one entire hour I stood between him and certain death. The boys would have killed him if they could have got by me.

By and by, when the company were far in the rear, I put away my pipe—I was getting fearfully dry and crisp about the gills and rather blown with good diligent work—and spurred my animated trance up alongside the Arab and stopped him and asked for water. He unslung his little gourd-shaped earthenware jug, and I put it under my moustache and took a long, glorious, satisfying draught. I was going to scour the mouth of the jug a little, but I saw that I had brought the whole train together once more by my delay, and that they were all anxious to drink too—and would have been long ago if the Arab had not pretended that he was out of water. So I hastened to pass the vessel to Davis. He took a mouthful, and never said a word, but climbed off his horse and lay down calmly in the road. I felt sorry for Davis. It was too late now, though, and Dan was drinking. Dan got down too, and hunted for a soft place. I thought I heard Dan say, "That Arab's friends ought to keep him in alcohol or else take him out and bury him somewhere." All the boys took a drink and climbed down. It is not well to go into further particulars. Let us draw the curtain upon this act.

....

Well, now, to think that after three changing years I should hear from that curious old relic again, and see Dan advertising it for sale for the benefit of a benevolent object. Dan is not treating that present right. I gave that pipe to him for a keepsake. However, he probably finds that it keeps away custom and interferes with business. It is the most convincing inanimate object in all this part of the world, perhaps. Dan and I were room-mates in all that long "Quaker City" voyage, and whenever I desired to have a little season of privacy I used to fire up on that pipe and persuade Dan to go out; and he seldom waited to change his clothes, either. In about a quarter, or from that to three-quarters of a minute, he would be propping up the smoke-stack on the upper deck and cursing. I wonder how the faithful old relic is going to sell?

A REMINISCENCE OF THE BACK SETTLEMENTS

"Now that corpse [said the undertaker, patting the folded hands of the deceased approvingly] was a brick—every way you took him he was a brick. He was so real accommodating, and so modest-like and simple in his last moments. Friends wanted metallic burial case—nothing else would do. I couldn't get it. There warn't going to be time—anybody could see that. Corpse said never mind, shake him up some kind of a box he could stretch out in comfortable, he warn't particular 'bout the general style of it. Said he went more on room than style, any way, in the last final container. Friends wanted a silver door-plate on the coffin, signifying who he was and wher' he was from. Now you know a fellow couldn't roust out such a gaily thing as that in a little country town like this. What did corpse say? Corpse said, whitewash his old canoe and dob his address and general destination onto it with a blacking brush and a stencil plate, long with a verse from some likely hymn or other, and p'int him for the tomb, and mark him C. O. D., and just let him skip along. He warn't distressed any more than you be—on the contrary just as carm and collected as a hearse-horse; said he judged that wher' he was going to, a body would find it considerable better to attract attention by a picturesque moral character than a natty burial case with a swell doorplate on it. Splendid man, he was. I'd druther do for a corpse like that 'n any I've tackled in seven year. There's some satisfaction in buryin' a man like that. You feel that what you're doing is appreciated. Lord bless you, so's he got planted before he sp'iled, he was perfectly satisfied; said his relations meant well, perfectly well, but all them preparations was bound to delay the thing more or less, and he didn't wish to be kept layin' round. You never see such a clear head as what he had—and so carm and so cool. Just a hunk of brains that is what he was. Perfectly awful. It was a ripping distance from one end of that man's head to t'other. Often and over again he's had brain fever a-raging in one place, and the rest of the pile didn't know anything about it—didn't affect it any more than an Injun insurrection in Arizona affects the Atlantic States. Well, the relations they wanted a big funeral, but corpse said he was down on flummery—didn't want any procession—fill the hearse full of mourners, and get out a stern line and tow him behind. He was the most down on style of any remains I ever struck. A beautiful, simple-minded creature—it was what he was, you can depend on that. He was just set on having things the way he wanted them, and he took a solid comfort in laying his little plans. He had me measure him and take a whole raft of directions; then he had a minister stand up behind a long box with a tablecloth over it and read his funeral sermon, saying 'Angcore, angcore!' at the good places, and making him scratch out every bit of brag about him, and all the hifalutin; and then he made them trot out the choir so's he could help them pick out the tunes for the occasion, and he got them to sing 'Pop Goes the Weasel,' because he'd always liked that tune when he was downhearted, and solemn music made him sad; and when they sung that with tears in their eyes (because they all loved him), and his relations grieving around, he just laid there as happy as a bug, and trying to beat time and showing all over how much he enjoyed it; and presently he got worked up and excited; and tried to join in, for mind you he was pretty proud of his abilities in the singing line; but the first time he opened his mouth and was just going to spread himself, his breath took a walk. I never see a man snuffed out so sudden. Ah, it was a great loss—it was a powerful loss to this poor little one-horse town. Well, well, well, I hain't got time to be palavering along here—got to nail on the lid and mosey along with' him; and if you'll just give me a lift we'll skeet him into the hearse and meander along. Relations bound to have it so—don't pay no attention to dying injunctions, minute a corpse's gone; but if I had my way, if I didn't respect his last wishes and tow him behind the hearse, I'll be cuss'd. I consider that whatever a corpse wants done for his comfort is a little enough matter, and a man hain't got no right to deceive him or take advantage of him—and whatever a corpse trusts me to do I'm a-going to do, you know, even if it's to stuff him and paint him yaller and keep him for a keepsake—you hear me!"

He cracked his whip and went lumbering away with his ancient ruin of a hearse, and I continued my walk with a valuable lesson learned—that a healthy and wholesome cheerfulness is not necessarily impossible to any occupation. The lesson is likely to be lasting, for it will take many months to obliterate the memory of the remarks and circumstances that impressed it.

A ROYAL COMPLIMENT

The latest report about the Spanish crown is, that it will now be offered to Prince Alfonso, the second son of the King of Portugal, who is but five years of age. The Spaniards have hunted through all the nations of Europe for a King. They tried to get a Portuguese in the person of Dom-Luis, who is an old ex-monarch; they tried to get an Italian, in the person of Victor Emanuel's young son, the Duke of Genoa; they tried to get a Spaniard, in the person of Espartero, who is an octogenarian. Some of them desired a French Bourbon, Montpensier; some of them a Spanish Bourbon, the Prince of Asturias; some of them an English prince, one of the sons of Queen Victoria. They have just tried to get the German Prince Leopold; but they have thought it better to give him up than take a war along with him. It is a long time since we first suggested to them to try an American ruler. We can offer them a large number of able and experienced sovereigns to pick from—men skilled in statesmanship, versed in the science of government, and adepts in all the arts of administration—men who could wear the crown with dignity and rule the kingdom at a reasonable expense.

There is not the least danger of Napoleon threatening them if they take an American sovereign; in fact, we have no doubt he would be pleased to support such a candidature. We are unwilling to mention names—though we have a man in our eye whom we wish they had in theirs.—New York Tribune.

It would be but an ostentation of modesty to permit such a pointed reference to myself to pass unnoticed. This is the second time that 'The Tribune' (no doubt sincerely looking to the best interests of Spain and the world at large) has done me the great and unusual honour to propose me as a fit person to fill the Spanish throne. Why 'The Tribune' should single me out in this way from the midst of a dozen Americans of higher political prominence, is a problem which I cannot solve. Beyond a somewhat intimate knowledge of Spanish history and a profound veneration for its great names and illustrious deeds, I feel that I possess no merit that should peculiarly recommend me to this royal distinction. I cannot deny that Spanish history has always been mother's milk to me. I am proud of every Spanish achievement, from Hernando Cortes's victory at Thermopylae down to Vasco Nunez de Balboa's discovery of the Atlantic ocean; and of every splendid Spanish name, from Don Quixote and the Duke of Wellington down to Don Caesar de Bazan. However, these little graces of erudition are of small consequence, being more showy than serviceable.

In case the Spanish sceptre is pressed upon me—and the indications unquestionably are that it will be—I shall feel it necessary to have certain things set down and distinctly understood beforehand. For instance: My salary must be paid quarterly in advance. In these unsettled times it will not do to trust. If Isabella had adopted this plan, she would be roosting on her ancestral throne to-day, for the simple reason that her subjects never could have raised three months of a royal salary in advance, and of course they could not have discharged her until they had squared up with her. My salary must be paid in gold; when greenbacks are fresh in a country, they are too fluctuating. My salary has got to be put at the ruling market rate; I am not going to cut under on the trade, and they are not going to trail me a long way from home and then practise on my ignorance and play me for a royal North Adams Chinaman, by any means. As I understand it, imported kings generally get five millions a year and house-rent free. Young George of Greece gets that. As the revenues only yield two millions, he has to take the national note for considerable; but even with things in that sort of shape he is better fixed than he was in Denmark, where he had to eternally stand up because he had no throne to sit on, and had to give bail for his board, because a royal apprentice gets no salary there while he is learning his trade. England is the place for that. Fifty thousand dollars a year Great Britain pays on each royal child that is born, and this is increased from year to year as the child becomes more and more indispensable to his country. Look at Prince Arthur. At first he only got the usual birth-bounty; but now that he has got so that he can dance, there is simply no telling what wages he gets.

I should have to stipulate that the Spanish people wash more and endeavour to get along with less quarantine. Do you know, Spain keeps her ports fast locked against foreign traffic three-fourths of each year, because one day she is scared about the cholera, and the next about the plague, and next the measles, next the hooping cough, the hives, and the rash? but she does not mind leonine leprosy and elephantiasis any more than a great and enlightened civilisation minds freckles. Soap would soon remove her anxious distress about foreign distempers. The reason arable land is so scarce in Spain is because the people squander so much of it on their persons, and then when they die it is improvidently buried with them.

I should feel obliged to stipulate that Marshal Serrano be reduced to the rank of constable, or even roundsman. He is no longer fit to be City Marshal. A man who refused to be king because he was too old and feeble, is ill qualified to help sick people to the station-house when they are armed and their form of delirium tremens is of the exuberant and demonstrative kind.

I should also require that a force be sent to chase the late Queen Isabella out of France. Her presence there can work no advantage to Spain, and she ought to be made to move at once; though, poor thing, she has been chaste enough heretofore—for a Spanish woman.

I should also require that—

I am at this moment authoritatively informed that "The Tribune" did not mean me, after all. Very well, I do not care two cents.

THE APPROACHING EPIDEMIC

One calamity to which the death of Mr. Dickens dooms this country has not awakened the concern to which its gravity entitles it. We refer to the fact that the nation is to be lectured to death and read to death all next winter, by Tom, Dick, and Harry, with poor lamented Dickens for a pretext. All the vagabonds who can spell will afflict the people with "readings" from Pickwick and Copperfield, and all the insignificants who have been ennobled by the notice of the great novelist or transfigured by his smile will make a marketable commodity of it now, and turn the sacred reminiscence to the practical use of procuring bread and butter. The lecture rostrums will fairly swarm with these fortunates. Already the signs of it are perceptible. Behold how the unclean creatures are wending toward the dead lion and gathering to the feast:

"Reminiscences of Dickens." A lecture. By John Smith, who heard him read eight times.

"Remembrances of Charles Dickens." A lecture. By John Jones, who saw him once in a street car and twice in a barber shop.

"Recollections of Mr. Dickens." A lecture. By John Brown, who gained a wide fame by writing deliriously appreciative critiques and rhapsodies upon the great author's public readings; and who shook hands with the great author upon various occasions, and held converse with him several times.

"Readings from Dickens." By John White, who has the great delineator's style and manner perfectly, having attended all his readings in this country and made these things a study, always practising each reading before retiring, and while it was hot from the great delineator's lips. Upon this occasion Mr. W. will exhibit the remains of a cigar which he saw Mr. Dickens smoke. This Relic is kept in a solid silver box made purposely for it.

"Sights and Sounds of the Great Novelist." A popular lecture. By John Gray, who waited on his table all the time he was at the Grand Hotel, New York, and still has in his possession and will exhibit to the audience a fragment of the Last Piece of Bread which the lamented author tasted in this country.

"Heart Treasures of Precious Moments with Literature's Departed Monarch." A lecture. By Miss Serena Amelia Tryphenia McSpadden, who still wears, and will always wear, a glove upon the hand made sacred by the clasp of Dickens. Only Death shall remove it.

"Readings from Dickens." By Mrs. J. O'Hooligan Murphy, who washed for him.

"Familiar Talks with the Great Author." A narrative lecture. By John Thomas, for two weeks his valet in America.

And so forth, and so on. This isn't half the list. The man who has a "Toothpick once used by Charles Dickens" will have to have a hearing; and the man who "once rode in an omnibus with Charles Dickens;" and the lady to whom Charles Dickens "granted the hospitalities of his umbrella during a storm;" and the person who "possesses a hole which once belonged in a handkerchief owned by Charles Dickens." Be patient and long-suffering, good people, for even this does not fill up the measure of what you must endure next winter. There is no creature in all this land who has had any personal relations with the late Mr. Dickens, however slight or trivial, but will shoulder his way to the rostrum and inflict his testimony upon his helpless countrymen. To some people it is fatal to be noticed by greatness.

THE TONE-IMPARTING COMMITTEE

When I get old and ponderously respectable, only one thing will be able to make me truly happy, and that will be to be put on the Venerable Tone-Imparting committee of the city of New York, and have nothing to do but sit on the platform, solemn and imposing, along with Peter Cooper, Horace Greeley, etc., etc., and shed momentary fame at second hand on obscure lecturers, draw public attention to lectures which would otherwise clack eloquently to sounding emptiness, and subdue audiences into respectful hearing of all sorts of unpopular and outlandish dogmas and isms. That is what I desire for the cheer and gratification of my gray hairs. Let me but sit up there with those fine relics of the Old Red Sandstone Period and give Tone to an intellectual entertainment twice a week, and be so reported, and my happiness will be complete. Those men have been my envy for a long, long time. And no memories of my life are so pleasant as my reminiscence of their long and honorable career in the Tone-imparting service. I can recollect that first time I ever saw them on the platforms just as well as I can remember the events of yesterday. Horace Greeley sat on the right, Peter Cooper on the left, and Thomas Jefferson, Red Jacket, Benjamin Franklin, and John Hancock sat between them. This was on the 22d of December, 1799, on the occasion of the state' funeral of George Washington in New York. It was a great day, that—a great day, and a very, very sad one. I remember that Broadway was one mass of black crape from Castle Garden nearly up to where the City Hall now stands. The next time I saw these gentlemen officiate was at a ball given for the purpose of procuring money and medicines for the sick and wounded soldiers and sailors. Horace Greeley occupied one side of the platform on which the musicians were exalted, and Peter Cooper the other. There were other Tone-imparters attendant upon the two chiefs, but I have forgotten their names now. Horace Greeley, gray-haired and beaming, was in sailor costume—white duck pants, blue shirt, open at the breast, large neckerchief, loose as an ox-bow, and tied with a jaunty sailor knot, broad turnover collar with star in the corner, shiny black little tarpaulin hat roosting daintily far back on head, and flying two gallant long ribbons. Slippers on ample feet, round spectacles on benignant nose, and pitchfork in hand, completed Mr. Greeley, and made him, in my boyish admiration, every inch a sailor, and worthy to be the honored great-grandfather of the Neptune he was so ingeniously representing. I shall never forget him. Mr. Cooper was dressed as a general of militia, and was dismally and oppressively warlike. I neglected to remark, in the proper place, that the soldiers and sailors in whose aid the ball was given had just been sent in from Boston—this was during the war of 1812. At the grand national reception of Lafayette, in 1824, Horace Greeley sat on the right and Peter Cooper to the left. The other Tone-imparters of the day are sleeping the sleep of the just now. I was in the audience when Horace Greeley, Peter Cooper, and other chief citizens imparted tone to the great meetings in favor of French liberty, in 1848. Then I never saw them any more until here lately; but now that I am living tolerably near the city, I run down every time I see it announced that "Horace Greeley, Peter Cooper, and several other distinguished citizens will occupy seats on the platform;" and next morning, when I read in the first paragraph of the phonographic report that "Horace Greeley, Peter Cooper, and several other distinguished citizens occupied seats on the platform," I say to myself, "Thank God, I was present." Thus I have been enabled to see these substantial old friends of mine sit on the platform and give tone to lectures on anatomy, and lectures on agriculture, and lectures on stirpiculture, and lectures on astronomy, on chemistry, on miscegenation, on "Is Man Descended from the Kangaroo?" on veterinary matters, on all kinds of religion, and several kinds of politics; and have seen them give tone and grandeur to the Four-legged Girl, the Siamese Twins, the Great Egyptian Sword Swallower, and the Old Original Jacobs. Whenever somebody is to lecture on a subject not of general interest, I know that my venerated Remains of the Old Red Sandstone Period will be on the platform; whenever a lecturer is to appear whom nobody has heard of before, nor will be likely to seek to see, I know that the real benevolence of my old friends will be taken advantage of, and that they will be on the platform (and in the bills) as an advertisement; and whenever any new and obnoxious deviltry in philosophy, morals, or politics is to be sprung upon the people, I know perfectly well that these intrepid old heroes will be on the platform too, in the interest of full and free discussion, and to crush down all narrower and less generous souls with the solid dead weight of their awful respectability. And let us all remember that while these inveterate and imperishable presiders (if you please) appear on the platform every night in the year as regularly as the volunteered piano from Steinway's or Chickering's, and have bolstered up and given tone to a deal of questionable merit and obscure emptiness in their time, they have also diversified this inconsequential service by occasional powerful uplifting and upholding of great progressive ideas which smaller men feared to meddle with or countenance.

OUR PRECIOUS LUNATIC

[From the Buffalo Express, Saturday, May 14, 1870.]

New YORK, May 10.

The Richardson-McFarland jury had been out one hour and fifty minutes. A breathless silence brooded over court and auditory—a silence and a stillness so absolute, notwithstanding the vast multitude of human beings packed together there, that when some one far away among the throng under the northeast balcony cleared his throat with a smothered little cough it startled everybody uncomfortably, so distinctly did it grate upon the pulseless air. At that imposing moment the bang of a door was heard, then the shuffle of approaching feet, and then a sort of surging and swaying disorder among the heads at the entrance from the jury-room told them that the Twelve were coming. Presently all was silent again, and the foreman of the jury rose and said:

"Your Honor and Gentleman: We, the jury charged with the duty of determining whether the prisoner at the bar, Daniel McFarland, has been guilty of murder, in taking by surprise an unarmed man and shooting him to death, or whether the prisoner is afflicted with a sad but irresponsible insanity which at times can be cheered only by violent entertainment with firearms, do find as follows, namely:

"That the prisoner, Daniel McFarland, is insane as above described. Because:

"1. His great grandfather's stepfather was tainted with insanity, and frequently killed people who were distasteful to him. Hence, insanity is hereditary in the family.

"2. For nine years the prisoner at the bar did not adequately support his family. Strong circumstantial evidence of insanity.

"3. For nine years he made of his home, as a general thing, a poor-house;

sometimes (but very rarely) a cheery, happy habitation; frequently the den of a beery, drivelling, stupefied animal; but never, as far as ascertained, the abiding place of a gentleman. These be evidences of insanity.

"4. He once took his young unmarried sister-in-law to the museum; while there his hereditary insanity came upon him to such a degree that he hiccupped and staggered; and afterward, on the way home, even made love to the young girl he was protecting. These are the acts of a person not in his right mind.

"5. For a good while his sufferings were so great that he had to submit to the inconvenience of having his wife give public readings for the family support; and at times, when he handed these shameful earnings to the barkeeper, his haughty soul was so torn with anguish that he could hardly stand without leaning against something. At such times he has been known to shed tears into his sustenance till it diluted to utter inefficiency. Inattention of this nature is not the act of a Democrat unafflicted in mind.

"6. He never spared expense in making his wife comfortable during her occasional confinements. Her father is able to testify to this. There was always an element of unsoundness about the prisoner's generosities that is very suggestive at this time and before this court.

"7. Two years ago the prisoner came fearlessly up behind Richardson in the dark, and shot him in the leg. The prisoner's brave and protracted defiance of an adversity that for years had left him little to depend upon for support but a wife who sometimes earned scarcely anything for weeks at a time, is evidence that he would have appeared in front of Richardson and shot him in the stomach if he had not been insane at the time of the shooting.

"8. Fourteen months ago the prisoner told Archibald Smith that he was going to kill Richardson. This is insanity.

"9. Twelve months ago he told Marshall P. Jones that he was going to kill Richardson. Insanity.

"10. Nine months ago he was lurking about Richardson's home in New Jersey, and said he was going to kill Richardson. Insanity.

"11. Seven months ago he showed a pistol to Seth Brown and said that that was for Richardson. He said Brown testified that at that time it seemed plain that something was the matter with McFarland, for he crossed the street diagonally nine times in fifty yards, apparently without any settled reason for doing so, and finally fell in the gutter and went to sleep. He remarked at the time that McFarland acted strange—believed he was insane. Upon hearing Brown's evidence, John W. Galen, M.D., affirmed at once that McFarland was insane.

"12. Five months ago, McFarland showed his customary pistol, in his customary way, to his bed-fellow, Charles A. Dana, and told him he was going to kill Richardson the first time an opportunity offered. Evidence of insanity.

"13. Five months and two weeks ago McFarland asked John Morgan the time of day, and turned and walked rapidly away without waiting for an answer. Almost indubitable evidence of insanity. And—

"14. It is remarkable that exactly one week after this circumstance, the prisoner, Daniel McFarland, confronted Albert D. Richardson suddenly and without warning, and shot him dead. This is manifest insanity. Everything we know of the prisoner goes to show that if he had been sane at the time, he would have shot his victim from behind.

"15. There is an absolutely overwhelming mass of testimony to show that an hour before the shooting, McFarland was ANXIOUS AND UNEASY, and that five minutes after it he was EXCITED. Thus the accumulating conjectures and evidences of insanity culminate in this sublime and unimpeachable proof of it. Therefore—

"Your Honor and Gentlemen—We the jury pronounce the said Daniel McFarland INNOCENT OF MURDER, BUT CALAMITOUSLY INSANE."

The scene that ensued almost defies description. Hats, handkerchiefs and bonnets were frantically waved above the massed heads in the courtroom, and three tremendous cheers and a tiger told where the sympathies of the court and people were. Then a hundred pursed lips were advanced to kiss the liberated prisoner, and many a hand thrust out to give him a congratulatory shake—but presto! with a maniac's own quickness and a maniac's own fury the lunatic assassin of Richardson fell upon his friends with teeth and nails, boots and office furniture, and the amazing rapidity with which he broke heads and limbs, and rent and sundered bodies, till nearly a hundred citizens were reduced to mere quivering heaps of fleshy odds and ends and crimson rags, was like nothing in this world but the exultant frenzy of a plunging, tearing, roaring devil of a steam machine when it snatches a human being and spins him and whirls him till he shreds away to nothingness like a "Four o'clock" before the breath of a child.

The destruction was awful. It is said that within the space of eight minutes McFarland killed and crippled some six score persons and tore down a large portion of the City Hall building, carrying away and casting into Broadway six or seven marble columns fifty-four feet long and weighing nearly two tons each. But he was finally captured and sent in chains to the lunatic asylum for life.

(By late telegrams it appears that this is a mistake.—Editor Express.)

But the really curious part of this whole matter is yet to be told. And that is, that McFarland's most intimate friends believe that the very next time that it ever occurred to him that the insanity plea was not a mere politic pretense, was when the verdict came in. They think that the startling thought burst upon him then, that if twelve good and true men, able to comprehend all the baseness of perjury, proclaimed under oath that he was a lunatic, there was no gainsaying such evidence and that he UNQUESTIONABLY WAS INSANE!

Possibly that was really the way of it. It is dreadful to think that maybe the most awful calamity that can befall a man, namely, loss of reason, was precipitated upon this poor prisoner's head by a jury that could have hanged him instead, and so done him a mercy and his country a service.

POSTSCRIPT-LATER

May 11—I do not expect anybody to believe so astounding a thing, and yet it is the solemn truth that instead of instantly sending the dangerous lunatic to the insane asylum (which I naturally supposed they would do, and so I prematurely said they had) the court has actually SET HIM AT LIBERTY. Comment is unnecessary. M. T.

THE EUROPEAN WARS

[From the Buffalo Express, July 25, 1870.]

First Day

THE EUROPEAN WAR!!!

NO BATTLE YET!!!

HOSTILITIES IMMINENT!!!

TREMENDOUS EXCITEMENT.

AUSTRIA ARMING!

BERLIN, Tuesday.

No battle has been fought yet. But hostilities may burst forth any week.

There is tremendous excitement here over news from the front that two companies of French soldiers are assembling there.

It is rumoured that Austria is arming—what with, is not known.

....

Second Day

THE EUROPEAN WAR

NO BATTLE YET!

FIGHTING IMMINENT.

AWFUL EXCITEMENT.

RUSSIA SIDES WITH PRUSSIA!

ENGLAND NEUTRAL!!

AUSTRIA NOT ARMING.

BERLIN, Wednesday.

No battle has been fought yet. However, all thoughtful men feel that the land may be drenched with blood before the Summer is over.

There is an awful excitement here over the rumour that two companies of Prussian troops have concentrated on the border. German confidence remains unshaken!!

There is news to the effect that Russia espouses the cause of Prussia and will bring 4,000,000 men to the field.

England proclaims strict neutrality.

The report that Austria is arming needs confirmation.

....

Third Day

THE EUROPEAN WAR

NO BATTLE YET!

BLOODSHED IMMINENT!!

ENORMOUS EXCITEMENT!!

INVASION OF PRUSSIA!!

INVASION OF FRANCE!!

RUSSIA SIDES WITH FRANCE.

ENGLAND STILL NEUTRAL!

FIRING HEARD!

THE EMPEROR TO TAKE COMMAND.

PARIS, Thursday.

No battle has been fought yet. But Field Marshal McMahon telegraphs thus to the Emperor:

"If the Frinch army survoives until Christmas there'll be throuble. Forninst this fact it would be sagacious if the divil wint the rounds of his establishment to prepare for the occasion, and tuk the precaution to warrum up the Prussian depairtment a bit agin the day. MIKE."

There is an enormous state of excitement here over news from the front to the effect that yesterday France and Prussia were simultaneously invaded by the two bodies of troops which lately assembled on the border. Both armies conducted their invasions secretly and are now hunting around for each other on opposite sides of the border.

Russia espouses the cause of France. She will bring 200,000 men to the field.

England continues to remain neutral.

Firing was heard yesterday in the direction of Blucherberg, and for a while the excitement was intense. However the people reflected that the country in that direction is uninhabitable, and impassable by anything but birds, they became quiet again.

The Emperor sends his troops to the field with immense enthusiasm. He will lead them in person, when they return.

....

Fourth Day

THE EUROPEAN WAR!

NO BATTLE YET!!

THE TROOPS GROWING OLD!

BUT BITTER STRIFE IMMINENT!

PRODIGIOUS EXCITEMENT!

THE INVASIONS SUCCESSFULLY ACCOMPLISHED

AND THE INVADERS SAFE!

RUSSIA SIDES WITH BOTH SIDES

ENGLAND WILL FIGHT BOTH!

LONDON, Friday.

No battle has been fought thus far, but a million impetuous soldiers are gritting their teeth at each other across the border, and the most serious fears entertained that if they do not die of old age first, there will be bloodshed in this war yet.

The prodigious patriotic excitement goes on. In Prussia, per Prussian telegrams, though contradicted from France. In France, per French telegrams, though contradicted from Prussia.

The Prussian invasion of France was a magnificent success. The military failed to find the French, but made good their return to Prussia without the loss of a single man. The French invasion of Prussia is also demonstrated to have been a brilliant and successful achievement. The army failed to find the Prussians, but made good their return to the Vaterland without bloodshed, after having invaded as much as they wanted to.

There is glorious news from Russia to the effect that she will side with both sides.

Also from England—she will fight both sides.

....

LONDON, Thursday evening.

I rushed over too soon. I shall return home on Tuesday's steamer and wait until the war begins. M. T.

THE WILD MAN INTERVIEWED

[From the Buffalo Express, September 18, 1869.]

There has been so much talk about the mysterious "wild man" out there in the West for some time, that I finally felt it was my duty to go out and interview him. There was something peculiarly and touchingly romantic about the creature and his strange actions, according to the newspaper reports. He was represented as being hairy, long-armed, and of great strength and stature; ugly and cumbrous; avoiding men, but appearing suddenly and unexpectedly to women and children; going armed with a club, but never molesting any creature, except sheep, or other prey; fond of eating and drinking, and not particular about the quality, quantity, or character of the beverages and edibles; living in the woods like a wild beast, but never angry; moaning, and sometimes howling, but never uttering articulate sounds.

Such was "Old Shep" as the papers painted him. I felt that the story of his life must be a sad one—a story of suffering, disappointment, and exile—a story of man's inhumanity to man in some shape or other—and I longed to persuade the secret from him.

....

"Since you say you are a member of the press," said the wild man, "I am willing to tell you all you wish to know. Bye and bye you will comprehend why it is that I wish to unbosom myself to a newspaper man when I have so studiously avoided conversation with other people. I will now unfold my strange story. I was born with the world we live upon, almost. I am the son of Cain."

"What?"

"I was present when the flood was announced."

"Which?"

"I am the father of the Wandering Jew."

"Sir?"

I moved out of range of his club, and went on taking notes, but keeping a wary eye on him all the while. He smiled a melancholy smile and resumed:

"When I glance back over the dreary waste of ages, I see many a glimmering and mark that is familiar to my memory. And oh, the leagues I have travelled! the things I have seen! the events I have helped to emphasise! I was at the assassination of Caesar. I marched upon Mecca with Mahomet. I was in the Crusades, and stood with Godfrey when he planted the banner of the cross on the battlements of Jerusalem. I—"

"One moment, please. Have you given these items to any other journal? Can I—"

"Silence. I was in the Pinta's shrouds with Columbus when America burst upon his vision. I saw Charles I beheaded. I was in London when the Gunpowder Plot was discovered. I was present at the trial of Warren Hastings. I was on American soil when the battle of Lexington was fought when the declaration was promulgated—when Cornwallis surrendered—When Washington died. I entered Paris with Napoleon after Elba. I was present when you mounted your guns and manned your fleets for the war of 1812—when the South fired upon Sumter—when Richmond fell—when the President's life was taken. In all the ages I have helped to celebrate the triumphs of genius, the achievements of arms, the havoc of storm, fire, pestilence, famine."

"Your career has been a stirring one. Might I ask how you came to locate in these dull Kansas woods, when you have been so accustomed to excitement during what I might term so protracted a period, not to put too fine a point on it?"

"Listen. Once I was the honoured servitor of the noble and illustrious" (here he heaved a sigh, and passed his hairy hand across his eyes) "but in these degenerate days I am become the slave of quack doctors and newspapers. I am driven from pillar to post and hurried up and down, sometimes with stencil-plate and paste-brush to defile the fences with cabalistic legends, and sometimes in grotesque and extravagant character at the behest of some driving journal. I attended to that Ocean Bank robbery some weeks ago, when I was hardly rested from finishing up the pow-wow about the completion of the Pacific Railroad; immediately I was spirited off to do an atrocious, murder for the benefit of the New York papers; next to attend the wedding of a patriarchal millionaire; next to raise a hurrah about the great boat race; and then, just when I had begun to hope that my old bones would have a rest, I am bundled off to this howling wilderness to strip, and jibber, and be ugly and hairy, and pull down fences and waylay sheep, and waltz around with a club, and play 'Wild Man' generally—and all to gratify the whim of a bedlam of crazy newspaper scribblers? From one end of the continent to the other, I am described as a gorilla, with a sort of human seeming about me—and all to gratify this quill-driving scum of the earth!"

"Poor old carpet bagger!"

"I have been served infamously, often, in modern and semi-modern times. I have been compelled by base men to create fraudulent history, and to perpetrate all sorts of humbugs. I wrote those crazy Junius letters, I moped in a French dungeon for fifteen years, and wore a ridiculous Iron Mask; I poked around your Northern forests, among your vagabond Indians, a solemn French idiot, personating the ghost of a dead Dauphin, that the gaping world might wonder if we had 'a Bourbon among us'; I have played sea-serpent off Nahant, and Woolly-Horse and What-is-it for the museums; I have interviewed politicians for the Sun, worked up all manner of miracles for the Herald, ciphered up election returns for the World, and thundered Political Economy through the Tribune. I have done all the extravagant things that the wildest invention could contrive, and done them well, and this is my reward—playing Wild Man in Kansas without a shirt!"

"Mysterious being, a light dawns vaguely upon me—it grows apace— what—what is your name."

"SENSATION!"

"Hence, horrible shape!"

It spoke again:

"Oh pitiless fate, my destiny hounds me once more. I am called. I go. Alas, is there no rest for me?"

In a moment the Wild Man's features seemed to soften and refine, and his form to assume a more human grace and symmetry. His club changed to a spade, and he shouldered it and started away sighing profoundly and shedding tears.

"Whither, poor shade?"

"TO DIG UP THE BYRON FAMILY!"

Such was the response that floated back upon the wind as the sad spirit shook its ringlets to the breeze, flourished its shovel aloft, and disappeared beyond the brow of the hill.

All of which is in strict accordance with the facts.

M. T.

LAST WORDS OF GREAT MEN

[From the Buffalo Express, September 11, 1889.]

Marshal Neil's last words were: "L'armee fran-caise!" (The French

army.)—Exchange.

What a sad thing it is to see a man close a grand career with a plagiarism in his mouth. Napoleon's last words were: "Tete d'armee." (Head of the army.) Neither of those remarks amounts to anything as "last words," and reflect little credit upon the utterers.

A distinguished man should be as particular about his last words as he is about his last breath. He should write them out on a slip of paper and take the judgment of his friends on them. He should never leave such a thing to the last hour of his life, and trust to an intellectual spirit at the last moment to enable him to say something smart with his latest gasp and launch into eternity with grandeur. No—a man is apt to be too much fagged and exhausted, both in body and mind, at such a time, to be reliable; and maybe the very thing he wants to say, he cannot think of to save him; and besides there are his weeping friends bothering around; and worse than all as likely as not he may have to deliver his last gasp before he is expecting to. A man cannot always expect to think of a natty thing to say under such circumstances, and so it is pure egotistic ostentation to put it off. There is hardly a case on record where a man came to his last moment unprepared and said a good thing—hardly a case where a man trusted to that last moment and did not make a solemn botch of it and go out of the world feeling absurd.

Now there was Daniel Webster. Nobody could tell him anything. He was not afraid. He could do something neat when the time came. And how did it turn out? Why, his will had to be fixed over; and then all the relations came; and first one thing and then another interfered, till at last he only had a chance to say, "I still live," and up he went.

Of course he didn't still live, because he died—and so he might as well have kept his last words to himself as to have gone and made such a failure of it as that. A week before that fifteen minutes of calm reflection would have enabled that man to contrive some last words that would have been a credit to himself and a comfort to his family for generations to come.

And there was John Quincy Adams. Relying on his splendid abilities and his coolness in emergencies, he trusted to a happy hit at the last moment to carry him through, and what was the result? Death smote him in the House of Representatives, and he observed, casually, "This is the last of earth." The last of earth! Why "the last of earth" when there was so much more left? If he had said it was the last rose of summer or the last run of shad, it would have had as much point in it. What he meant to say was, "Adam was the first and Adams is the last of earth," but he put it off a trifle too long, and so he had to go with that unmeaning observation on his lips.

And there we have Napoleon's "Tete d'armee." That don't mean anything. Taken by itself, "Head of the army," is no more important than "Head of the police." And yet that was a man who could have said a good thing if he had barred out the doctor and studied over it a while. Marshal Neil, with half a century at his disposal, could not dash off anything better in his last moments than a poor plagiarism of another man's words, which were not worth plagiarizing in the first place. "The French army." Perfectly irrelevant—perfectly flat—utterly pointless. But if he had closed one eye significantly, and said, "The subscriber has made it lively for the French army," and then thrown a little of the comic into his last gasp, it would have been a thing to remember with satisfaction all the rest of his life. I do wish our great men would quit saying these flat things just at the moment they die. Let us have their next-to-the-last words for a while, and see if we cannot patch up from them something that will be more satisfactory.

The public does not wish to be outraged in this way all the time.

But when we come to call to mind the last words of parties who took the trouble to make the proper preparation for the occasion, we immediately notice a happy difference in the result.

There was Chesterfield. Lord Chesterfield had laboured all his life to build up the most shining reputation for affability and elegance of speech and manners the world has ever seen. And could you suppose he failed to appreciate the efficiency of characteristic "last words," in the matter of seizing the successfully driven nail of such a reputation and clinching on the other side for ever? Not he. He prepared himself. He kept his eye on the clock and his finger on his pulse. He awaited his chance. And at last, when he knew his time was come, he pretended to think a new visitor had entered, and so, with the rattle in his throat emphasised for dramatic effect, he said to the servant, "Shin around, John, and get the gentleman a chair." And so he died, amid thunders of applause.

Next we have Benjamin Franklin. Franklin, the author of Poor Richard's quaint sayings; Franklin the immortal axiom-builder, who used to sit up at nights reducing the rankest old threadbare platitudes to crisp and snappy maxims that had a nice, varnished, original look in their regimentals; who said, "Virtue is its own reward;" who said, "Procrastination is the thief of time;" who said, "Time and tide wait for no man" and "Necessity is the mother of invention;" good old Franklin, the Josh Billings of the eighteenth century—though, sooth to say, the latter transcends him in proverbial originality as much as he falls short of him in correctness of orthography. What sort of tactics did Franklin pursue? He pondered over his last words for as much as two weeks, and then when the time came, he said, "None but the brave deserve the fair," and died happy. He could not have said a sweeter thing if he had lived till he was an idiot.

Byron made a poor business of it, and could not think of anything to say, at the last moment but, "Augusta—sister—Lady Byron—tell Harriet Beecher Stowe"—etc., etc.,—but Shakespeare was ready and said, "England expects every man to do his duty!" and went off with splendid eclat.

And there are other instances of sagacious preparation for a felicitous closing remark. For instance:

Joan of Arc said, "Tramp, tramp, tramp the boys are marching."

Alexander the Great said, "Another of those Santa Cruz punches, if you please."

The Empress Josephine said, "Not for Jo-" and could get no further.

Cleopatra said, "The Old Guard dies, but never surrenders."

Sir Walter Raleigh said, "Executioner, can I take your whetstone a moment, please?" though what for is not clear.

John Smith said, "Alas, I am the last of my race."

Queen Elizabeth said, "Oh, I would give my kingdom for one moment more—I have forgotten my last words."

And Red Jacket, the noblest Indian brave that ever wielded a tomahawk in defence of a friendless and persecuted race, expired with these touching words upon his lips,

"Wawkawampanoosucwinnebayowallazvsagamoresa-skatchewan."

There was not a dry eye in the wigwam.

Let not this lesson be lost upon our public men. Let them take a healthy moment for preparation, and contrive some last words that shall be neat and to the point. Let Louis Napoleon say,

"I am content to follow my uncle—still, I do not wish to improve upon his last word. Put me down for 'Tete d'armee.'"

And Garret Davis, "Let me recite the unabridged dictionary."

And H. G., "I desire, now, to say a few words on political economy."

And Mr. Bergh, "Only take part of me at a time, if the load will be fatiguing to the hearse horses."

And Andrew Johnson, "I have been an alderman, Member of Congress, Governor, Senator, Pres—adieu, you know the rest."

And Seward., "Alas!-ka."

And Grant, "O."

All of which is respectfully submitted, with the most honorable intentions. M. T.

P. S.—I am obliged to leave out the illustrations. The artist finds it impossible to make a picture of people's last words.

About Author

Samuel Langhorne Clemens (November 30, 1835 – April 21, 1910), known by his pen name Mark Twain, was an American writer, humorist, entrepreneur, publisher, and lecturer. He was lauded as the "greatest humorist this country has produced", and William Faulkner called him "the father of American literature". His novels include The Adventures of Tom Sawyer (1876) and its sequel, the Adventures of Huckleberry Finn (1884), the latter often called "The Great American Novel".

Twain was raised in Hannibal, Missouri, which later provided the setting for Tom Sawyer and Huckleberry Finn. He served an apprenticeship with a printer and then worked as a typesetter, contributing articles to the newspaper of his older brother Orion Clemens. He later became a riverboat pilot on the Mississippi River before heading west to join Orion in Nevada. He referred humorously to his lack of success at mining, turning to journalism for the Virginia City Territorial Enterprise. His humorous story, "The Celebrated Jumping Frog of Calaveras County", was published in 1865, based on a story that he heard at Angels Hotel in Angels Camp, California, where he had spent some time as a miner. The short story brought international attention and was even translated into French. His wit and satire, in prose and in speech, earned praise from critics and peers, and he was a friend to presidents, artists, industrialists, and European royalty.

Twain earned a great deal of money from his writings and lectures, but he invested in ventures that lost most of it—such as the Paige Compositor, a mechanical typesetter that failed because of its complexity and imprecision. He filed for bankruptcy in the wake of these financial setbacks, but he eventually overcame his financial troubles with the help of Henry Huttleston Rogers. He eventually paid all his creditors in full, even though his bankruptcy relieved him of having to do so.

Twain was born shortly after an appearance of Halley's Comet, and he predicted that he would "go out with it" as well; he died the day after the comet returned.

Biography

Early life

Samuel Langhorne Clemens was born on November 30, 1835, in Florida, Missouri, the sixth of seven children born to Jane (née Lampton; 1803–1890), a native of Kentucky, and John Marshall Clemens (1798–1847), a native of Virginia. His parents met when his father moved to Missouri, and they were married in 1823. Twain was of Cornish, English, and Scots-Irish descent. Only three of his siblings survived childhood: Orion (1825–1897), Henry (1838–1858), and Pamela (1827–1904). His sister Margaret (1830–1839) died when Twain was three, and his brother Benjamin (1832–1842) died three years later. His brother Pleasant Hannibal (1828) died at three weeks of age.

When he was four, Twain's family moved to Hannibal, Missouri, a port town on the Mississippi River that inspired the fictional town of St. Petersburg in The Adventures of Tom Sawyer and the Adventures of Huckleberry Finn. Slavery was legal in Missouri at the time, and it became a theme in these writings. His father was an attorney and judge, who died of pneumonia in 1847, when Twain was 11. The next year, Twain left school after the fifth grade to become a printer's apprentice. In 1851, he began working as a typesetter, contributing articles and humorous sketches to the Hannibal Journal, a newspaper that Orion owned. When he was 18, he left Hannibal and worked as a printer in New York City, Philadelphia, St. Louis, and Cincinnati, joining the newly formed International Typographical Union, the printers trade union. He educated himself in public libraries in the evenings, finding wider information than at a conventional school.

Twain describes his boyhood in Life on the Mississippi, stating that "there was but one permanent ambition" among his comrades: to be a steamboatman.

Pilot was the grandest position of all. The pilot, even in those days of trivial wages, had a princely salary – from a hundred and fifty to two hundred and fifty dollars a month, and no board to pay.

68

As Twain describes it, the pilot's prestige exceeded that of the captain. The pilot had to:

...get up a warm personal acquaintanceship with every old snag and one-limbed cottonwood and every obscure wood pile that ornaments the banks of this river for twelve hundred miles; and more than that, must... actually know where these things are in the dark

Steamboat pilot Horace E. Bixby took Twain on as a cub pilot to teach him the river between New Orleans and St. Louis for $500 (equivalent to $14,000 in 2018), payable out of Twain's first wages after graduating. Twain studied the Mississippi, learning its landmarks, how to navigate its currents effectively, and how to read the river and its constantly shifting channels, reefs, submerged snags, and rocks that would "tear the life out of the strongest vessel that ever floated". It was more than two years before he received his pilot's license. Piloting also gave him his pen name from "mark twain", the leadsman's cry for a measured river depth of two fathoms (12 feet), which was safe water for a steamboat.

As a young pilot, Clemens served on the steamer A. B. Chambers with Grant Marsh, who became famous for his exploits as a steamboat captain on the Missouri River. The two liked each other, and admired one another, and maintained a correspondence for many years after Clemens left the river.

While training, Samuel convinced his younger brother Henry to work with him, and even arranged a post of mud clerk for him on the steamboat Pennsylvania. On June 13, 1858, the steamboat's boiler exploded; Henry succumbed to his wounds on June 21. Twain claimed to have foreseen this death in a dream a month earlier, which inspired his interest in parapsychology; he was an early member of the Society for Psychical Research. Twain was guilt-stricken and held himself responsible for the rest of his life. He continued to work on the river and was a river pilot until the Civil War broke out in 1861, when traffic was curtailed along the Mississippi River. At the start of hostilities, he enlisted briefly in a local Confederate unit. He later wrote the sketch "The Private History of a Campaign That Failed", describing how he and his friends had been Confederate volunteers for two weeks before disbanding.

He then left for Nevada to work for his brother Orion, who was Secretary of the Nevada Territory. Twain describes the episode in his book Roughing It.

Travels

Orion became secretary to Nevada Territory governor James W. Nye in 1861, and Twain joined him when he moved west. The brothers traveled more than two weeks on a stagecoach across the Great Plains and the Rocky Mountains, visiting the Mormon community in Salt Lake City.

Twain's journey ended in the silver-mining town of Virginia City, Nevada, where he became a miner on the Comstock Lode. He failed as a miner and went to work at the Virginia City newspaper Territorial Enterprise, working under a friend, the writer Dan DeQuille. He first used his pen name here on February 3, 1863, when he wrote a humorous travel account entitled "Letter From Carson – re: Joe Goodman; party at Gov. Johnson's; music" and signed it "Mark Twain".

His experiences in the American West inspired Roughing It, written during 1870–71 and published in 1872. His experiences in Angels Camp (in Calaveras County, California) provided material for "The Celebrated Jumping Frog of Calaveras County" (1865).

Twain moved to San Francisco in 1864, still as a journalist, and met writers such as Bret Harte and Artemus Ward. He may have been romantically involved with the poet Ina Coolbrith.

His first success as a writer came when his humorous tall tale "The Celebrated Jumping Frog of Calaveras County" was published on November 18, 1865, in the New York weekly The Saturday Press, bringing him national attention. A year later, he traveled to the Sandwich Islands (present-day Hawaii) as a reporter for the Sacramento Union. His letters to the Union were popular and became the basis for his first lectures.

In 1867, a local newspaper funded his trip to the Mediterranean aboard the Quaker City, including a tour of Europe and the Middle East. He wrote a collection of travel letters which were later compiled as The Innocents Abroad (1869). It was on this trip that he met fellow passenger Charles Langdon, who showed him a picture of his sister Olivia. Twain later claimed to have fallen in love at first sight.

Upon returning to the United States, Twain was offered honorary membership in Yale University's secret society Scroll and Key in 1868. Its devotion to "fellowship, moral and literary self-improvement, and charity" suited him well.

Marriage and children

Twain and Olivia Langdon corresponded throughout 1868. She rejected his first marriage proposal, but they were married in Elmira, New York in February 1870, where he courted her and managed to overcome her father's initial reluctance. She came from a "wealthy but liberal family"; through her, he met abolitionists, "socialists, principled atheists and activists for women's rights and social equality", including Harriet Beecher Stowe (his next-door neighbor in Hartford, Connecticut), Frederick Douglass, and writer and utopian socialist William Dean Howells, who became a long-time friend. The couple lived in Buffalo, New York, from 1869 to 1871. He owned a stake in the Buffalo Express newspaper and worked as an editor and writer. While they were living in Buffalo, their son Langdon died of diphtheria at the age of 19 months. They had three daughters: Susy (1872–1896), Clara (1874–1962), and Jean (1880–1909).

Twain moved his family to Hartford, Connecticut, where he arranged the building of a home starting in 1873. In the 1870s and 1880s, the family summered at Quarry Farm in Elmira, the home of Olivia's sister, Susan Crane. In 1874, Susan had a study built apart from the main house so that Twain would have a quiet place in which to write. Also, he smoked cigars constantly, and Susan did not want him to do so in her house.

Twain wrote many of his classic novels during his 17 years in Hartford (1874–1891) and over 20 summers at Quarry Farm. They include The Adventures of Tom Sawyer (1876), The Prince and the Pauper (1881), Life on the Mississippi (1883), Adventures of Huckleberry Finn (1884), and A

Connecticut Yankee in King Arthur's Court (1889).

The couple's marriage lasted 34 years until Olivia's death in 1904. All of the Clemens family are buried in Elmira's Woodlawn Cemetery.

Love of science and technology

Twain was fascinated with science and scientific inquiry. He developed a close and lasting friendship with Nikola Tesla, and the two spent much time together in Tesla's laboratory.

Twain patented three inventions, including an "Improvement in Adjustable and Detachable Straps for Garments" (to replace suspenders) and a history trivia game. Most commercially successful was a self-pasting scrapbook; a dried adhesive on the pages needed only to be moistened before use. Over 25,000 were sold.

Twain was an early proponent of fingerprinting as a forensic technique, featuring it in a tall tale in Life on the Mississippi (1883) and as a central plot element in the novel Pudd'nhead Wilson (1894).

Twain's novel A Connecticut Yankee in King Arthur's Court (1889) features a time traveler from the contemporary U.S., using his knowledge of science to introduce modern technology to Arthurian England. This type of historical manipulation became a trope of speculative fiction as alternate histories.

In 1909, Thomas Edison visited Twain at his home in Redding, Connecticut and filmed him. Part of the footage was used in The Prince and the Pauper (1909), a two-reel short film. It is the only known existing film footage of Twain.

Financial troubles

Twain made a substantial amount of money through his writing, but he lost a great deal through investments. He invested mostly in new inventions and technology, particularly the Paige typesetting machine. It was a beautifully engineered mechanical marvel that amazed viewers when it worked, but it was prone to breakdowns. Twain spent $300,000 (equal to $9,000,000 in inflation-adjusted terms) on it between 1880 and 1894, but before it could be perfected it was rendered obsolete by the Linotype. He lost the bulk of his book profits, as well as a substantial portion of his wife's inheritance.

Twain also lost money through his publishing house, Charles L. Webster and Company, which enjoyed initial success selling the memoirs of Ulysses S. Grant but failed soon afterward, losing money on a biography of Pope Leo XIII. Fewer than 200 copies were sold.

Twain and his family closed down their expensive Hartford home in response to the dwindling income and moved to Europe in June 1891. William M. Laffan of The New York Sun and the McClure Newspaper Syndicate offered him the publication of a series of six European letters. Twain, Olivia, and their daughter Susy were all faced with health problems, and they believed that it would be of benefit to visit European baths. The family stayed mainly in France, Germany, and Italy until May 1895, with longer spells at Berlin (winter 1891/92), Florence (fall and winter 1892/93), and Paris (winters and springs 1893/94 and 1894/95). During that period, Twain returned four times to New York due to his enduring business troubles. He took "a cheap room" in September 1893 at $1.50 per day (equivalent to $42 in 2018) at The Players Club, which he had to keep until March 1894; meanwhile, he became "the Belle of New York," in the words of biographer Albert Bigelow Paine.

Twain's writings and lectures enabled him to recover financially, combined with the help of his friend, Henry Huttleston Rogers. He began a friendship with the financier in 1893, a principal of Standard Oil, that lasted the remainder of his life. Rogers first made him file for bankruptcy in April 1894, then had him transfer the copyrights on his written works to his wife to prevent creditors from gaining possession of them. Finally, Rogers took absolute charge of Twain's money until all his creditors were paid.

Twain accepted an offer from Robert Sparrow Smythe and embarked on a year-long, around the world lecture tour in July 1895 to pay off his creditors in full, although he was no longer under any legal obligation to do so. It was a long, arduous journey and he was sick much of the time, mostly from a cold and a carbuncle. The first part of the itinerary took him across northern America to British Columbia, Canada, until the second half of August. For the second part, he sailed across the Pacific Ocean. His scheduled lecture in Honolulu, Hawaii had to be canceled due to a cholera epidemic. Twain went on to Fiji, Australia, New Zealand, Sri Lanka, India, Mauritius, and South Africa. His three months in India became the centerpiece of his 712-page book Following the Equator. In the second half of July 1896, he sailed back to England, completing his circumnavigation of the world begun 14 months before.

Twain and his family spent four more years in Europe, mainly in England and Austria (October 1897 to May 1899), with longer spells in London and Vienna. Clara had wished to study the piano under Theodor Leschetizky in Vienna. However, Jean's health did not benefit from consulting with specialists in Vienna, the "City of Doctors". The family moved to London in spring 1899, following a lead by Poultney Bigelow who had a good experience being treated by Dr. Jonas Henrik Kellgren, a Swedish osteopathic practitioner in Belgravia. They were persuaded to spend the summer at Kellgren's sanatorium by the lake in the Swedish village of Sanna. Coming back in fall, they continued the treatment in London, until Twain was convinced by lengthy inquiries in America that similar osteopathic expertise was available there.

In mid-1900, he was the guest of newspaper proprietor Hugh Gilzean-Reid at Dollis Hill House, located on the north side of London. Twain wrote that he had "never seen any place that was so satisfactorily situated, with its noble trees and stretch of country, and everything that went to make life delightful, and all within a biscuit's throw of the metropolis of the world." He then returned to America in October 1900, having earned enough to pay off his debts. In winter 1900/01, he became his country's most prominent opponent of imperialism, raising the issue in his speeches, interviews, and writings. In January 1901, he began serving as vice-president of the Anti-Imperialist League of New York.

Speaking engagements

Twain was in great demand as a featured speaker, performing solo humorous talks similar to modern stand-up comedy. He gave paid talks to many men's clubs, including the Authors' Club, Beefsteak Club, Vagabonds, White Friars, and Monday Evening Club of Hartford.

In the late 1890s, he spoke to the Savage Club in London and was elected an honorary member. He was told that only three men had been so honored, including the Prince of Wales, and he replied: "Well, it must make the Prince feel mighty fine." He visited Melbourne and Sydney in 1895 as part of a world lecture tour. In 1897, he spoke to the Concordia Press Club in Vienna as a special guest, following the diplomat Charlemagne Tower, Jr. He delivered the speech "Die Schrecken der Deutschen Sprache" ("The Horrors of the German Language")—in German—to the great amusement of the audience. In 1901, he was invited to speak at Princeton University's Cliosophic Literary Society, where he was made an honorary member.

Canadian visits

In 1881, Twain was honored at a banquet in Montreal, Canada where he made reference to securing a copyright. In 1883, he paid a brief visit to Ottawa, and he visited Toronto twice in 1884 and 1885 on a reading tour with George Washington Cable, known as the "Twins of Genius" tour.

The reason for the Toronto visits was to secure Canadian and British copyrights for his upcoming book Adventures of Huckleberry Finn, to which he had alluded in his Montreal visit. The reason for the Ottawa visit had been to secure Canadian and British copyrights for Life on the Mississippi. Publishers in Toronto had printed unauthorized editions of his books at the time, before an international copyright agreement was established in 1891. These were sold in the United States as well as in Canada, depriving him of royalties. He estimated that Belford Brothers' edition of The Adventures of Tom Sawyer alone had cost him ten thousand dollars (equivalent to $280,000 in 2018). He had unsuccessfully attempted to secure the rights for The Prince and the Pauper in 1881, in conjunction with his Montreal trip. Eventually, he received legal advice to register a copyright in Canada (for both Canada and Britain) prior to publishing in the United States, which would restrain the Canadian publishers from printing a version when the American edition was published. There was a requirement that a copyright be registered to a Canadian resident; he addressed this by his short visits to the country.

Later life and death

... the report is greatly exaggerated.

—Twain's reaction to a report of his death

Twain lived in his later years at 14 West 10th Street in Manhattan. He passed through a period of deep depression which began in 1896 when his daughter Susy died of meningitis. Olivia's death in 1904 and Jean's on December 24, 1909, deepened his gloom. On May 20, 1909, his close friend Henry Rogers died suddenly. In 1906, Twain began his autobiography in the North American Review. In April, he heard that his friend Ina Coolbrith had lost nearly all that she owned in the 1906 San Francisco earthquake, and he volunteered a few autographed portrait photographs to be sold for her benefit. To further aid Coolbrith, George Wharton James visited Twain in New York and arranged for a new portrait session. He was resistant initially, but he eventually admitted that four of the resulting images were the finest ones ever taken of him.

Twain formed a club in 1906 for girls whom he viewed as surrogate granddaughters called the Angel Fish and Aquarium Club. The dozen or so members ranged in age from 10 to 16. He exchanged letters with his "Angel Fish" girls and invited them to concerts and the theatre and to play games. Twain wrote in 1908 that the club was his "life's chief delight". In 1907, he met Dorothy Quick (aged 11) on a transatlantic crossing, beginning "a friendship that was to last until the very day of his death".

Oxford University awarded Twain an honorary doctorate in letters in 1907.

Twain was born two weeks after Halley's Comet's closest approach in 1835; he said in 1909:

I came in with Halley's Comet in 1835. It is coming again next year, and I expect to go out with it. It will be the greatest disappointment of my life if

I don't go out with Halley's Comet. The Almighty has said, no doubt: "Now here are these two unaccountable freaks; they came in together, they must go out together".

Twain's prediction was accurate; he died of a heart attack on April 21, 1910, in Redding, Connecticut, one day after the comet's closest approach to Earth.

Upon hearing of Twain's death, President William Howard Taft said:

Mark Twain gave pleasure – real intellectual enjoyment – to millions, and his works will continue to give such pleasure to millions yet to come … His humor was American, but he was nearly as much appreciated by Englishmen and people of other countries as by his own countrymen. He has made an enduring part of American literature.

Twain's funeral was at the Brick Presbyterian Church on Fifth Avenue, New York. He is buried in his wife's family plot at Woodlawn Cemetery in Elmira, New York. The Langdon family plot is marked by a 12-foot monument (two fathoms, or "mark twain") placed there by his surviving daughter Clara. There is also a smaller headstone. He expressed a preference for cremation (for example, in Life on the Mississippi), but he acknowledged that his surviving family would have the last word.

Officials in Connecticut and New York estimated the value of Twain's estate at $471,000 ($13,000,000 today).

Writing

Overview

Twain began his career writing light, humorous verse, but he became a chronicler of the vanities, hypocrisies, and murderous acts of mankind. At mid-career, he combined rich humor, sturdy narrative, and social criticism in Huckleberry Finn. He was a master of rendering colloquial speech and helped to create and popularize a distinctive American literature built on American themes and language.

Many of his works have been suppressed at times for various reasons. The

Adventures of Huckleberry Finn has been repeatedly restricted in American high schools, not least for its frequent use of the word "nigger", which was in common usage in the pre-Civil War period in which the novel was set.

A complete bibliography of Twain's works is nearly impossible to compile because of the vast number of pieces he wrote (often in obscure newspapers) and his use of several different pen names. Additionally, a large portion of his speeches and lectures have been lost or were not recorded; thus, the compilation of Twain's works is an ongoing process. Researchers rediscovered published material as recently as 1995 and 2015.

Early journalism and travelogues

Twain was writing for the Virginia City newspaper the Territorial Enterprise in 1863 when he met lawyer Tom Fitch, editor of the competing newspaper Virginia Daily Union and known as the "silver-tongued orator of the Pacific". He credited Fitch with giving him his "first really profitable lesson" in writing. "When I first began to lecture, and in my earlier writings," Twain later commented, "my sole idea was to make comic capital out of everything I saw and heard." In 1866, he presented his lecture on the Sandwich Islands to a crowd in Washoe City, Nevada. Afterwards, Fitch told him:

Clemens, your lecture was magnificent. It was eloquent, moving, sincere. Never in my entire life have I listened to such a magnificent piece of descriptive narration. But you committed one unpardonable sin – the unpardonable sin. It is a sin you must never commit again. You closed a most eloquent description, by which you had keyed your audience up to a pitch of the intensest interest, with a piece of atrocious anti-climax which nullified all the really fine effect you had produced.

It was in these days that Twain became a writer of the Sagebrush School; he was known later as its most famous member. His first important work was "The Celebrated Jumping Frog of Calaveras County," published in the New York Saturday Press on November 18, 1865. After a burst of popularity, the Sacramento Union commissioned him to write letters about his travel experiences. The first journey that he took for this job was to ride the steamer Ajax on its maiden voyage to the Sandwich Islands (Hawaii).

All the while, he was writing letters to the newspaper that were meant for publishing, chronicling his experiences with humor. These letters proved to be the genesis to his work with the San Francisco Alta California newspaper, which designated him a traveling correspondent for a trip from San Francisco to New York City via the Panama isthmus.

On June 8, 1867, he set sail on the pleasure cruiser Quaker City for five months, and this trip resulted in The Innocents Abroad or The New Pilgrims' Progress. In 1872, he published his second piece of travel literature, Roughing It, as an account of his journey from Missouri to Nevada, his subsequent life in the American West, and his visit to Hawaii. The book lampoons American and Western society in the same way that Innocents critiqued the various countries of Europe and the Middle East. His next work was The Gilded Age: A Tale of Today, his first attempt at writing a novel. The book, written with his neighbor Charles Dudley Warner, is also his only collaboration.

Twain's next work drew on his experiences on the Mississippi River. Old Times on the Mississippi was a series of sketches published in the Atlantic Monthly in 1875 featuring his disillusionment with Romanticism. Old Times eventually became the starting point for Life on the Mississippi.

Tom Sawyer and Huckleberry Finn

Twain's next major publication was The Adventures of Tom Sawyer, which draws on his youth in Hannibal. Tom Sawyer was modeled on Twain as a child, with traces of schoolmates John Briggs and Will Bowen. The book also introduces Huckleberry Finn in a supporting role, based on Twain's boyhood friend Tom Blankenship.

The Prince and the Pauper was not as well received, despite a storyline that is common in film and literature today. The book tells the story of two boys born on the same day who are physically identical, acting as a social commentary as the prince and pauper switch places. Twain had started Adventures of Huckleberry Finn (which he consistently had problems completing) and had completed his travel book A Tramp Abroad, which describes his travels through central and southern Europe.

Twain's next major published work was the Adventures of Huckleberry Finn, which confirmed him as a noteworthy American writer. Some have called it the first Great American Novel, and the book has become required reading in many schools throughout the United States. Huckleberry Finn was an offshoot from Tom Sawyer and had a more serious tone than its predecessor. Four hundred manuscript pages were written in mid-1876, right after the publication of Tom Sawyer. The last fifth of Huckleberry Finn is subject to much controversy. Some say that Twain experienced a "failure of nerve," as critic Leo Marx puts it. Ernest Hemingway once said of Huckleberry Finn:

If you read it, you must stop where the Nigger Jim is stolen from the boys. That is the real end. The rest is just cheating.

Hemingway also wrote in the same essay:

All modern American literature comes from one book by Mark Twain called Huckleberry Finn.

Near the completion of Huckleberry Finn, Twain wrote Life on the Mississippi, which is said to have heavily influenced the novel. The travel work recounts Twain's memories and new experiences after a 22-year absence from the Mississippi River. In it, he also explains that "Mark Twain" was the call made when the boat was in safe water, indicating a depth of two fathoms (12 feet or 3.7 metres).

Later writing

Twain produced President Ulysses S. Grant's Memoirs through his fledgling publishing house, Charles L. Webster & Company, which he co-owned with Charles L. Webster, his nephew by marriage.

At this time he also wrote "The Private History of a Campaign That Failed" for The Century Magazine. This piece detailed his two-week stint in a Confederate militia during the Civil War. He next focused on A Connecticut Yankee in King Arthur's Court, written with the same historical fiction style as The Prince and the Pauper. A Connecticut Yankee showed the absurdities of political and social norms by setting them in the court of King Arthur. The book was started in December 1885, then shelved a few months later until the summer of 1887, and eventually finished in the spring of 1889.

His next large-scale work was Pudd'nhead Wilson, which he wrote rapidly, as he was desperately trying to stave off bankruptcy. From November 12 to December 14, 1893, Twain wrote 60,000 words for the novel. Critics[who?] have pointed to this rushed completion as the cause of the novel's rough organization and constant disruption of the plot. This novel also contains the tale of two boys born on the same day who switch positions in life, like The Prince and the Pauper. It was first published serially in Century Magazine and, when it was finally published in book form, Pudd'nhead Wilson appeared as the main title; however, the "subtitles" make the entire title read: The Tragedy of Pudd'nhead Wilson and the Comedy of The Extraordinary Twins.

Twain's next venture was a work of straight fiction that he called Personal Recollections of Joan of Arc and dedicated to his wife. He had long said[where?] that this was the work that he was most proud of, despite the criticism that he received for it. The book had been a dream of his since childhood, and he claimed that he had found a manuscript detailing the life of Joan of Arc when he was an adolescent. This was another piece that he was convinced would save his publishing company. His financial adviser Henry Huttleston Rogers quashed that idea and got Twain out of that business altogether, but the book was published nonetheless.[citation needed]

To pay the bills and keep his business projects afloat, Twain had begun to write articles and commentary furiously, with diminishing returns, but it was not enough. He filed for bankruptcy in 1894. During this time of dire financial straits, he published several literary reviews in newspapers to help make ends meet. He famously derided James Fenimore Cooper in his article detailing Cooper's "Literary Offenses". He became an extremely outspoken critic of other authors and other critics; he suggested that, before praising Cooper's work, Thomas Lounsbury, Brander Matthews, and Wilkie Collins "ought to have read some of it".

George Eliot, Jane Austen, and Robert Louis Stevenson also fell under Twain's attack during this time period, beginning around 1890 and continuing until his death. He outlines what he considers to be "quality writing" in several letters and essays, in addition to providing a source for the "tooth and claw" style of literary criticism. He places emphasis on concision, utility of word choice, and realism; he complains, for example, that Cooper's Deerslayer purports to be realistic but has several shortcomings. Ironically, several of his own works were later criticized for lack of continuity (Adventures of Huckleberry Finn) and organization (Pudd'nhead Wilson).

Twain's wife died in 1904 while the couple were staying at the Villa di Quarto in Florence. After some time had passed he published some works that his wife, his de facto editor and censor throughout her married life, had looked down upon. The Mysterious Stranger is perhaps the best known, depicting various visits of Satan to earth. This particular work was not published in Twain's lifetime. His manuscripts included three versions, written between 1897 and 1905: the so-called Hannibal, Eseldorf, and Print Shop versions. The resulting confusion led to extensive publication of a jumbled version, and only recently have the original versions become available as Twain wrote them.

Twain's last work was his autobiography, which he dictated and thought would be most entertaining if he went off on whims and tangents in non-chronological order. Some archivists and compilers have rearranged the biography into a more conventional form, thereby eliminating some of Twain's humor and the flow of the book. The first volume of the autobiography, over 736 pages, was published by the University of California in November 2010, 100 years after his death, as Twain wished. It soon became an unexpected best-seller, making Twain one of a very few authors publishing new best-selling volumes in the 19th, 20th, and 21st centuries.

Censorship

Twain's works have been subjected to censorship efforts. According to Stuart (2013), "Leading these banning campaigns, generally, were religious organizations or individuals in positions of influence – not so much working librarians, who had been instilled with that American "library spirit" which honored intellectual freedom (within bounds of course)". In 1905, the Brooklyn Public Library banned both The Adventures of Huckleberry Finn and The Adventures of Tom Sawyer from the children's department because of their language.

Views

Twain's views became more radical as he grew older. In a letter to friend and fellow writer William Dean Howells in 1887 he acknowledged that his views had changed and developed over his lifetime, referring to one of his favorite works:

When I finished Carlyle's French Revolution in 1871, I was a Girondin; every time I have read it since, I have read it differently – being influenced and changed, little by little, by life and environment ... and now I lay the book down once more, and recognize that I am a Sansculotte! And not a pale, characterless Sansculotte, but a Marat.

Anti-imperialist

Before 1899, Twain was an ardent imperialist. In the late 1860s and early 1870s, he spoke out strongly in favor of American interests in the Hawaiian Islands. He said the war with Spain in 1898 was "the worthiest" war ever fought. In 1899, however, he reversed course. In the New York Herald, October 16, 1900, Twain describes his transformation and political awakening, in the context of the Philippine–American War, to anti-imperialism:

I wanted the American eagle to go screaming into the Pacific ... Why not spread its wings over the Philippines, I asked myself? ... I said to myself, Here are a people who have suffered for three centuries. We can make them as free as ourselves, give them a government and country of their own, put a miniature of the American Constitution afloat in the Pacific, start a brand new republic to take its place among the free nations of the world. It seemed to me a great task to which we had addressed ourselves.

But I have thought some more, since then, and I have read carefully the treaty of Paris [which ended the Spanish–American War], and I have seen that we do not intend to free, but to subjugate the people of the Philippines. We have gone there to conquer, not to redeem.

It should, it seems to me, be our pleasure and duty to make those people free, and let them deal with their own domestic questions in their own way. And so I am an anti-imperialist. I am opposed to having the eagle put its talons on any other land.

During the Boxer rebellion, Twain said that "the Boxer is a patriot. He loves his country better than he does the countries of other people. I wish him success."

From 1901, soon after his return from Europe, until his death in 1910, Twain was vice-president of the American Anti-Imperialist League, which opposed the annexation of the Philippines by the United States and had "tens of thousands of members". He wrote many political pamphlets for the organization. The Incident in the Philippines, posthumously published in 1924, was in response to the Moro Crater Massacre, in which six hundred Moros were killed. Many of his neglected and previously uncollected writings on anti-imperialism appeared for the first time in book form in 1992.

Twain was critical of imperialism in other countries as well. In Following the Equator, Twain expresses "hatred and condemnation of imperialism of all stripes". He was highly critical of European imperialists, such as Cecil Rhodes, who greatly expanded the British Empire, and Leopold II, King of the Belgians. King Leopold's Soliloquy is a stinging political satire about his private colony, the Congo Free State. Reports of outrageous exploitation and grotesque abuses led to widespread international protest in the early 1900s, arguably the first large-scale human rights movement. In the soliloquy, the King argues that bringing Christianity to the country outweighs a little starvation. Leopold's rubber gatherers were tortured, maimed and slaughtered until the movement forced Brussels to call a halt.

During the Philippine–American War, Twain wrote a short pacifist story titled The War Prayer, which makes the point that humanism and Christianity's preaching of love are incompatible with the conduct of war. It was submitted to Harper's Bazaar for publication, but on March 22, 1905, the magazine rejected the story as "not quite suited to a woman's magazine". Eight days later, Twain wrote to his friend Daniel Carter Beard, to whom he had read the story, "I don't think the prayer will be published in my time. None but the dead are permitted to tell the truth." Because he had an exclusive contract with Harper & Brothers, Twain could not publish The War Prayer elsewhere; it remained unpublished until 1923. It was republished as campaigning material by Vietnam War protesters.

Twain acknowledged that he had originally sympathized with the more moderate Girondins of the French Revolution and then shifted his sympathies to the more radical Sansculottes, indeed identifying himself as "a Marat" and writing that the Reign of Terror paled in comparison to the older terrors that preceded it. Twain supported the revolutionaries in Russia against the reformists, arguing that the Tsar must be got rid of by violent means, because peaceful ones would not work. He summed up his views of revolutions in the following statement:

I am said to be a revolutionist in my sympathies, by birth, by breeding and by principle. I am always on the side of the revolutionists, because there never was a revolution unless there were some oppressive and intolerable conditions against which to revolute.

Civil rights

Twain was an adamant supporter of the abolition of slavery and the emancipation of slaves, even going so far as to say, "Lincoln's Proclamation ... not only set the black slaves free, but set the white man free also". He argued that non-whites did not receive justice in the United States, once saying, "I have seen Chinamen abused and maltreated in all the mean, cowardly ways possible to the invention of a degraded nature ... but I never saw a Chinaman righted in a court of justice for wrongs thus done to him". He paid for at least one black person to attend Yale Law School and for another black person to attend a southern university to become a minister.

Twain's sympathetic views on race were not reflected in his early writings on American Indians. Of them, Twain wrote in 1870:

His heart is a cesspool of falsehood, of treachery, and of low and devilish instincts. With him, gratitude is an unknown emotion; and when one does him a kindness, it is safest to keep the face toward him, lest the reward be an arrow in the back. To accept of a favor from him is to assume a debt which you can never repay to his satisfaction, though you bankrupt yourself trying. The scum of the earth!

As counterpoint, Twain's essay on "The Literary Offenses of Fenimore Cooper" offers a much kinder view of Indians. "No, other Indians would have noticed these things, but Cooper's Indians never notice anything. Cooper thinks they are marvelous creatures for noticing, but he was almost always in error about his Indians. There was seldom a sane one among them." In his later travelogue Following the Equator (1897), Twain observes that in colonized lands all over the world, "savages" have always been wronged by "whites" in the most merciless ways, such as "robbery, humiliation, and slow, slow murder, through poverty and the white man's whiskey"; his conclusion is that "there are many humorous things in this world; among them the white man's notion that he is less savage than the other savages". In an expression that captures his East Indian experiences, he wrote, "So far as I am able to judge nothing has been left undone, either by man or Nature, to make India the most extraordinary country that the sun visits on his rounds. Where every prospect pleases, and only man is vile."

Twain was also a staunch supporter of women's rights and an active campaigner for women's suffrage. His "Votes for Women" speech, in which he pressed for the granting of voting rights to women, is considered one of the most famous in history.

Helen Keller benefited from Twain's support as she pursued her college education and publishing despite her disabilities and financial limitations. The two were friends for roughly 16 years.

Through Twain's efforts, the Connecticut legislature voted a pension for Prudence Crandall, since 1995 Connecticut's official heroine, for her efforts towards the education of African-American young ladies in Connecticut. Twain also offered to purchase for her use her former house in Canterbury, home of the Canterbury Female Boarding School, but she declined.

Labor

Twain wrote glowingly about unions in the river boating industry in *Life on the Mississippi*, which was read in union halls decades later. He supported the labor movement, especially one of the most important unions, the Knights of Labor. In a speech to them, he said:

Who are the oppressors? The few: the King, the capitalist, and a handful of other overseers and superintendents. Who are the oppressed? The many: the nations of the earth; the valuable personages; the workers; they that make the bread that the soft-handed and idle eat.

Religion

Twain was a Presbyterian. He was critical of organized religion and certain elements of Christianity through his later life. He wrote, for example, "Faith is believing what you know ain't so", and "If Christ were here now there is one thing he would not be – a Christian". With anti-Catholic sentiment rampant in 19th century America, Twain noted he was "educated to enmity toward everything that is Catholic". As an adult, he engaged in religious discussions and attended services, his theology developing as he wrestled with the deaths of loved ones and with his own mortality.

Twain generally avoided publishing his most controversial opinions on religion in his lifetime, and they are known from essays and stories that were published later. In the essay Three Statements of the Eighties in the 1880s, Twain stated that he believed in an almighty God, but not in any messages, revelations, holy scriptures such as the Bible, Providence, or retribution in the afterlife. He did state that "the goodness, the justice, and the mercy of God are manifested in His works", but also that "the universe is governed by strict and immutable laws", which determine "small matters", such as who dies in a pestilence. At other times, he wrote or spoke in ways that contradicted a strict deist view, for example, plainly professing a belief in Providence. In some later writings in the 1890s, he was less optimistic about the goodness of God, observing that "if our Maker is all-powerful for good or evil, He is not in His right mind". At other times, he conjectured sardonically that perhaps God had created the world with all its tortures for some purpose of His own, but was otherwise indifferent to humanity, which was too petty and insignificant to deserve His attention anyway.

In 1901, Twain criticized the actions of the missionary Dr. William Scott Ament (1851–1909) because Ament and other missionaries had collected indemnities from Chinese subjects in the aftermath of the Boxer Uprising of 1900. Twain's response to hearing of Ament's methods was published in the North American Review in February 1901: To the Person Sitting in Darkness, and deals with examples of imperialism in China, South Africa, and with the U.S. occupation of the Philippines. A subsequent article, "To My Missionary Critics" published in The North American Review in April 1901, unapologetically continues his attack, but with the focus shifted from Ament to his missionary superiors, the American Board of Commissioners for Foreign Missions.

After his death, Twain's family suppressed some of his work that was especially irreverent toward conventional religion, including Letters from the Earth, which was not published until his daughter Clara reversed her position in 1962 in response to Soviet propaganda about the withholding. The anti-religious The Mysterious Stranger was published in 1916. Little Bessie, a story ridiculing Christianity, was first published in the 1972 collection Mark Twain's Fables of Man.

He raised money to build a Presbyterian Church in Nevada in 1864.

Twain created a reverent portrayal of Joan of Arc, a subject over which he had obsessed for forty years, studied for a dozen years and spent two years writing about. In 1900 and again in 1908 he stated, "I like Joan of Arc best of all my books, it is the best".

Those who knew Twain well late in life recount that he dwelt on the subject of the afterlife, his daughter Clara saying: "Sometimes he believed death ended everything, but most of the time he felt sure of a life beyond."

Twain's frankest views on religion appeared in his final work Autobiography of Mark Twain, the publication of which started in November 2010, 100 years after his death. In it, he said:

There is one notable thing about our Christianity: bad, bloody, merciless, money-grabbing, and predatory as it is – in our country particularly and in all other Christian countries in a somewhat modified degree – it is still a hundred times better than the Christianity of the Bible, with its prodigious crime – the invention of Hell. Measured by our Christianity of to-day, bad as it is, hypocritical as it is, empty and hollow as it is, neither the Deity nor his Son is a Christian, nor qualified for that moderately high place. Ours is a terrible religion. The fleets of the world could swim in spacious comfort in the innocent blood it has spilled.

Twain was a Freemason. He belonged to Polar Star Lodge No. 79 A.F.&A.M., based in St. Louis. He was initiated an Entered Apprentice on May 22, 1861, passed to the degree of Fellow Craft on June 12, and raised to the degree of Master Mason on July 10.

Twain visited Salt Lake City for two days and met there members of The Church of Jesus Christ of Latter-day Saints. They also gave him a Book of Mormon. He later wrote in Roughing It about that book:

The book seems to be merely a prosy detail of imaginary history, with the Old Testament for a model; followed by a tedious plagiarism of the New Testament.

Vivisection

Twain was opposed to the vivisection practices of his day. His objection was not on a scientific basis but rather an ethical one. He specifically cited the pain caused to the animal as his basis of his opposition:

I am not interested to know whether Vivisection produces results that are profitable to the human race or doesn't. ... The pains which it inflicts upon unconsenting animals is the basis of my enmity towards it, and it is to me sufficient justification of the enmity without looking further.

Pen names

Twain used different pen names before deciding on "Mark Twain". He signed humorous and imaginative sketches as "Josh" until 1863. Additionally, he used the pen name "Thomas Jefferson Snodgrass" for a series of humorous letters.

He maintained that his primary pen name came from his years working on Mississippi riverboats, where two fathoms, a depth indicating water safe for the passage of boat, was a measure on the sounding line. Twain is an archaic term for "two", as in "The veil of the temple was rent in twain." The riverboatman's cry was "mark twain" or, more fully, "by the mark twain", meaning "according to the mark [on the line], [the depth is] two [fathoms]", that is, "The water is 12 feet (3.7 m) deep and it is safe to pass."

Twain said that his famous pen name was not entirely his invention. In Life on the Mississippi, he wrote:

Captain Isaiah Sellers was not of literary turn or capacity, but he used to jot down brief paragraphs of plain practical information about the river, and sign them "MARK TWAIN", and give them to the New Orleans Picayune. They related to the stage and condition of the river, and were accurate and valuable; ... At the time that the telegraph brought the news of his death, I was on the Pacific coast. I was a fresh new journalist, and needed a nom de guerre; so I confiscated the ancient mariner's discarded one, and have done my best to make it remain what it was in his hands – a sign and symbol and warrant that whatever is found in its company may be gambled on as being the petrified truth; how I have succeeded, it would not be modest in me to say.

Twain's story about his pen name has been questioned by some with the suggestion that "mark twain" refers to a running bar tab that Twain would regularly incur while drinking at John Piper's saloon in Virginia City, Nevada. Samuel Clemens himself responded to this suggestion by saying, "Mark Twain was the nom de plume of one Captain Isaiah Sellers, who used to write river news over it for the New Orleans Picayune. He died in 1869 and as he could no longer need that signature, I laid violent hands upon it without asking permission of the proprietor's remains. That is the history of the nom de plume I bear."

In his autobiography, Twain writes further of Captain Sellers' use of "Mark Twain":

I was a cub pilot on the Mississippi River then, and one day I wrote a rude and crude satire which was leveled at Captain Isaiah Sellers, the oldest steamboat pilot on the Mississippi River, and the most respected, esteemed, and revered. For many years he had occasionally written brief paragraphs concerning the river and the changes which it had undergone under his observation during fifty years, and had signed these paragraphs "Mark Twain" and published them in the St. Louis and New Orleans journals. In my satire I made rude game of his reminiscences. It was a shabby poor performance, but I didn't know it, and the pilots didn't know it. The pilots thought it was brilliant. They were jealous of Sellers, because when the gray-heads among them pleased their vanity by detailing in the hearing of the younger craftsmen marvels which they had seen in the long ago on the river, Sellers was always likely to step in at the psychological moment and snuff them out with wonders of his own which made their small marvels look pale and sick. However, I have told all about this in "Old Times on the Mississippi." The pilots handed my extravagant satire to a river reporter, and it was published in the New Orleans True Delta. That poor old Captain Sellers was deeply wounded. He had never been held up to ridicule before; he was sensitive, and he never got over the hurt which I had wantonly and stupidly inflicted upon his dignity. I was proud of my performance for a while, and considered it quite wonderful, but I have changed my opinion of it long ago. Sellers never published another paragraph nor ever used his nom de guerre again.

Legacy and depictions

Trademark white suit

While Twain is often depicted wearing a white suit, modern representations suggesting that he wore them throughout his life are unfounded. Evidence suggests that Twain began wearing white suits on the lecture circuit, after the death of his wife Olivia ("Livy") in 1904. However, there is also evidence showing him wearing a white suit before 1904. In 1882, he sent a photograph of himself in a white suit to 18-year-old Edward W. Bok, later publisher of the Ladies Home Journal, with a handwritten dated note. The white suit did eventually become his trademark, as illustrated in anecdotes about this eccentricity (such as the time he wore a white summer suit to a Congressional hearing during the winter). McMasters' The Mark Twain Encyclopedia states that Twain did not wear a white suit in his last three years, except at one banquet speech.

In his autobiography, Twain writes of his early experiments with wearing white out-of-season:

Next after fine colors, I like plain white. One of my sorrows, when the summer ends, is that I must put off my cheery and comfortable white clothes and enter for the winter into the depressing captivity of the shapeless and degrading black ones. It is mid-October now, and the weather is growing cold up here in the New Hampshire hills, but it will not succeed in freezing me out of these white garments, for here the neighbors are few, and it is only of crowds that I am afraid. (Source: Wikipedia)

9 789389 682656